Wild Edges

Rachel Marie Chase

Published by Wild Edge Press, 2020.

This is a work of fiction. Similarities to real people, places, or events are entirely coincidental.

WILD EDGES

First edition. February 14, 2020.

ISBN: 978-1393358367

Written by Rachel Marie Chase.

Thank you to the dozens of readers who helped me refine this story and encouraged me to finish.

Thank you to my husband, who selflessly encourages me to follow my dreams and makes pancakes for the kids while I write.

Thank you to my kids, who are endlessly inspiring and only a little mad they aren't allowed to read this book.

Thank you to my Creator who gave me Everything.

To all those walking in darkness.

To all those who have seen a Great
Light.

To all those walking in the land of the
shadow of death.

Note to Reader

THROUGHOUT THIS STORY, you will find words, situations and individuals that may offend the traditional Christian worldview, but can easily be found all around us — maybe you even identify with them yourself. Just as you would in real life, I urge you to stick with the story and these characters until the very end.

Where can I go from your Spirit?
Where can I flee from your presence?
If I go up to the heavens, you are there;
if I make my bed in the depths, you are there.
If I rise on the wings of the dawn,
if I settle on the far side of the sea,
even there your hand will guide me,
your right hand will hold me fast.
If I say, "Surely the darkness will hide me
and the light become night around me,"
even the darkness will not be dark to you;
the night will shine like the day,
for darkness is as light to you.

Chapter 1

• • • •

IT HADN'T EVEN BEEN twenty-four hours. Kelsey glanced over at the slick bench seat next to him as the rumble of the engine faded into a pleasant background noise. The seat was empty now, but her presence was palpable. She would always be with him, just like her momma.

...

It had been hotter than usual the previous day... The late-summer air flowed in oppressive waves through the cab of the truck, gently lifting luminous chestnut strands of Annalee's hair. They caressed her petal pink cheeks and tickled her full rose lips. She reached up with a graceful hand to tuck the unruly pieces behind her ear. Kelsey caught a glance from her bright green eyes before she turned her gaze back to the open desert that spread endlessly around them.

He watched her bare toes, painted neon pink, tap on the faded peeling blue dashboard of his twenty-eight-year-old truck. He smiled as he heard the tinny country music playing softly on the radio, the words as familiar to him as the sound of the 1992 Ford F-150's engine.

Come on, he thought, let's get Little Darlin' there safe.

His sun-browned fingers gripped the worn steering wheel tightly as he adjusted his foot on the gas pedal. He glanced toward her again, this time catching her eyes. He smirked.

4

"*Daddy, why do you keep looking at me?*" she said, her voice light and unperturbed. A small smile played at the corner of her lips.

"*Just soaking it all in, Annie.*" His voice was deeper than he expected, emotion spilling into his words without consent.

Her sharp green eyes turned full on him. She had caught his emotion. Annalee Campbell had a sixth sense for the feelings of others and had been that way since birth. Her daddy was familiar with this scrutiny and shrugged it off.

"*Daddy...*" she began accusingly.

"*I'm fine, Annie.*" He smiled, but kept his eyes on the road, afraid they would betray him. "*You sound so much like your momma when you are about to lecture me.*"

He heard her let out a heavy breath. "*Don't you bring Momma into this. I told you I was worried about you.*" She paused. "*I don't have to do this, Daddy. I mean it.*"

Hearing his daughters genuine concern, his wave of emotion changed to determination. His voice was firm as he spoke this time, "*And Little Darlin', I told you that I will be just fine. A full ride to a big university is nothing to take lightly. This is an opportunity that your momma and I could have only dreamed of. A few tears from your daddy aren't going to keep you from that.*"

He felt her study on his face, calculating. Finally, she looked back out the window. He glanced her way again. She was thinking, her fingers idly rubbing together like they did when she was seriously considering something. Her eyes scanned the sage and dirt that flew by, not really seeing them.

"*Save all that thinking for school.*" He tried to lighten his tone as he reached over to brush his thumb against her cheek.

She turned back to him, as stubborn as he was, and unphased by his attempt to lift her mood. "I'm going to be checking on you every day, alright? You better keep your phone on you." Her tone betrayed her emotion as well.

"I will," he said simply and seriously. This seemed to satisfy her and they sat in companionable silence for a few miles.

Her voice was lighter when she spoke again.

"Why did you insist on driving this rust bucket? I don't even think it will make it to Tempe. We could've brought my Mustang. At least it would've got better gas mileage." Kelsey smiled, because, despite the derogatory reference to his truck, he knew she wouldn't want him to drive anything else.

"Your Mustang is a relic now, nearly eleven years older than this truck. Besides, you know this truck as well as I do. If something breaks down, we'll fix it together, just like we always have." He smiled widely, briefly picturing her at five years old, her tiny brown head lying next to his under the truck as he showed her how to drain the oil.

She was her momma's girl through and through, but when it came to cars, she had her daddy's heart and mechanic brain. When she began speaking in full sentences at age two, she started questioning the mechanics of the cars her daddy worked on at his shop. Thrilled to have his daughter so interested in his work, Kelsey involved her with everything. She would never take his word for how the cars were fixed, always demanding to see it for herself. She slowed down work for him considerably when she was little, but as she got into her teenage years, she was an invaluable helper. He could trust her with anything that came through the shop.

"You are going to be an amazing engineer, Little Darlin.'" She rolled her eyes at him as he spoke. "You wait and see. The best Arizona State has ever seen."

She let out a puff of laughter from her lips. "Oh, Daddy," she said and shook her head.

"I can just see your momma smiling right now." Moisture filled his eyes. He blinked away the vision of green eyes, so similar to those of the young woman sitting next to him.

He saw the corner of Annalee's mouth twitch down. "I know, Daddy." She swallowed hard. "She would've loved this drive. We never made it down to Phoenix. We were going to go when I graduated." Her voice remained steady. "Remember how she liked to roll all the windows down and sing as loud as she could with the radio on full blast?"

Kelsey and Annalee laughed together, low chuckles and bright giggles filling the cab. The happy sound hung in the air, thick as the summer heat.

Kelsey cleared his throat and cast a sidelong glance toward his daughter. "Now, about the boys."

Annalee laughed short and loud. "God, Daddy, it's 2020, do we really have to talk about boys?"

He held out a hand, signaling her to wait. "Now hold on. All I want to say..."

"Here we go." She settled into her seat and smirked.

He snorted. "As I was saying... If some boy comes around that looks or acts anything like your daddy, I want you to run. Run far and don't look back."

"Oh, Daddy. You couldn't have been that bad at my age."

Kelsey raised one thick brown eyebrow and clenched his teeth together. "I'm just trying to save you a lot of trouble."

She paused, considering. "Well, I appreciate your concern, but I don't think you have anything to worry about."

One quick glance at his beautiful daughter shed serious doubt on that statement, but he kept his mouth shut. He did have to give her credit for turning down every boy who had approached her in high school. And there were many. But she'd always said the boys weren't smart enough, handsome enough or didn't know enough about cars.

He smiled in spite of his genuine concern. "I do trust you, Annie. It's just hard to let go."

She didn't speak. Instead, she shifted her body on the seat, brought her feet onto the middle of the bench and leaned back against the passenger door. Her hair billowed up behind her head like flames. A shadow passed through her eyes and her lips settled into stillness. Her fingers began rubbing together again. Her eyes flicked to his and she took a breath.

"We've never talked about you and Momma and all that happened." She spoke quietly and slowly. The gravity in her words betrayed the significance of this topic for her. She'd obviously wanted to talk about it for quite some time.

Kelsey had known the questions would eventually come. He'd counted on her momma to answer them, knowing that he wouldn't say the right things in the right way or perhaps that he might not be able to say anything at all. A part of him wanted to tell her with all his heart. He wanted to share that which had made him who he was today. But mostly, he was terrified. If he talked to Annalee about the past, she would experience it as if it were her own. And he had spent the last twenty years protecting his baby girl from all of that. An involuntary breath shuddered through his lungs.

Her gaze fell into her lap as she spoke again. "It's okay. Momma said you wouldn't want to talk about it. She said some memories are too hard to speak out loud." Kelsey felt his throat tighten. Fresh tears filled his eyes. He looked up into the sky pleadingly. Annalee continued, "She told me some stuff, you know. Like what she was before. And about...about your dad."

Kelsey nodded, waiting for the tightness in his throat to loosen.

"I just want you to know that I'm grown up now, Daddy. And when you feel like you want to talk about everything, I'm here." He met her eyes. Maturity older than her nineteen years shone from them. He nodded again.

After a few minutes, Kelsey's throat cleared, but his voice was still choked as he spoke. "I...I guess that I'm not ready just yet." A small nervous chuckle escaped through his clenched jaw. "I'm sorry I'm not a better man, Little Darlin'. But I'm just not ready."

"I understand. I love you." Her voice was quiet but sure. She smiled reassuringly at him. "You've always left the talking to Momma." Kelsey chuckled again.

"It's been a pretty quiet year and a half since Momma left, huh?" Kelsey said.

"It has. But that's okay too," Annalee replied.

"Just how did you get so smart?" He grabbed her toes playfully as she wiggled her foot back and forth. "It was definitely not from your daddy."

"You got that right," she said, giggling as she lightly kicked his hand away.

...

The drive to Arizona State University from Beatty, Nevada, had taken just under seven hours. They had arrived in time for freshman orientation, spent the rest of the day getting Annalee's few possessions settled into her dorm room, and then headed out to a Mexican restaurant for dinner. Aside from a few mostly harmless reminders that her momma would have stayed for longer than one night, Kelsey felt that she was well settled and safe when he left the next morning.

In truth, leaving his daughter at school was one of the hardest things he had done in his life. Annalee was capable and ready, but leaving behind his only love on earth had proved to be more difficult than he'd been able to tolerate, and he'd looked forward to the long drive home to think and heal.

The drive proved to be pleasantly uneventful and left plenty of time for Kelsey to process the weekend's events. The familiar buildings that surrounded his hometown of Beatty surprised him when he started to recognize his surroundings. Seven hours had flown by, but he didn't feel quite ready to go home yet, and, as if on autopilot, he pulled into a long driveway south of town.

The new owners had taken good care of the place. Annalee's momma would've been happy about that. He closed his eyes and pictured Annalee's momma and her sister standing on the front porch waving goodbye, the breeze mingling their chocolate brown hair as they brought their heads together. They had loved each other dearly.

Another memory of the same porch formed. This time Annalee's momma was carrying boxes down the steps: the last few possessions her sister had owned. Her sister's sudden death from a congenital heart defect at the age of eighteen pulled the state financial support their mother received. With no children at home and a drug habit to support, their mother had sold the trailer just two days after her youngest daughter's death. She'd disappeared, leaving her oldest daughter to pick up the pieces. They'd never heard from her again.

Kelsey whipped the truck around, afraid of where the memories might lead him. Dust filled the cab through his open windows, swirling into his nostrils as he barreled toward the highway.

Low buildings and empty gravel parking lots lined the highway that doubled as main street in Beatty, Nevada. He absently noted each business until he drove by his own auto mechanic shop. It looked like Seth had opened up that morning and had a few cars in. Kelsey thought about turning in but wasn't ready for work just yet.

The road was straight and the town small, so he was at the edge within two minutes. A small grocery market stood at the end of town. To anyone else, the market was insignificant. To Kelsey, it was dynamite. As he drove by, he kept a practiced eye on the road, just as he had for the past year and a half. He hadn't so much as looked at the market since that fateful day. Just past it, Kelsey pushed hard on the gas pedal. The '92 sped up and sailed north.

Something was settling into his bones — a slowly building awareness that he had been ignoring for the last twenty-four hours. It had increased in intensity so much it couldn't be ignored. The something was driving him north toward his childhood, toward his past. He couldn't see, taste or smell it, but it was there. It split him in two and felt like death and life, love and hate, his past and present.

Sweat dripped from his nose and ran down his neck. Tears fell from his eyes and joined with the sweat, staining his dusky grey t-shirt black. The moisture spread like blood from a puncture wound to his chest. The hot air smothered him, his breath coming shallow and quick. The dust dried his mouth until his lips stuck to his teeth and his tongue felt like cotton.

His vision started to blur. He slammed his foot on the brake, vaguely registering the squeal of his tires as he came to a skidding stop on the side of the highway.

The dust settled in the cab, leaving a light film over everything by the time Kelsey took a full breath. It settled on his drenched skin and face too, forming a sticky grimy layer. Kelsey opened one eye to find that it had partially sealed shut from the salt and sweat. He tried opening his mouth but found it still too dry.

He didn't know how long he sat there, but a cool breeze mercifully began to blow through the truck. With the breeze, his breaths came easier. And with those breaths came clarity.

It was obvious what he needed to do.

The world around him faded away as he allowed his memories to carry him back twenty years, to driving the same truck on the same highway. Leaning his head against the seat, he closed his eyes and allowed himself to remember.

Chapter 2

• • • •

KELSEY PRESSED THE pedal hard against the floorboard. The rough gas engine of the his eight-year-old Ford F-150 protested with a deep grumbling rumble. The speed dial moved joltingly up to the 90 mph tick. The temperature gage at the gas station he'd passed had read 105 degrees. Air blew through the open window like a blast heater, whipping his tousled hair against his face. The stinging sensation was small distraction. He couldn't help staring at the Desert Rose Angels sign, even as he tried to get past it as fast as he could. His right hand gripped the black worn leather of the steering wheel while his left he took a long drag from his half-smoked cigarette. The pink border of the sign quickly faded behind him in his rearview mirror. He smashed the cigarette out in the dusty ash tray and ran his fingers through his hair. He sighed a smoky exhale and let off the gas slightly. The engine responded by graciously lowering its decibel level.

He shifted himself on the slick bench seat. The heated faux leather added to the warmth he was becoming increasingly aware of between his legs. The growing presence was a sickening reminder of his unconventional teenage life. If only he didn't know what it was like, that fleeting but intense pleasure of a woman. If he didn't, he would watch the sign go by with innocent curiosity. Instead, he looked at it with a solid knowl-

13

edge of what awaited any willing soul that ventured inside: the promise of touch, the feeling of belonging, the sweet hot release from life. It beckoned him, hitting him as hard as the summer wind blasting through his window.

Damn Brad, he thought and not for the first time. *Didn't he want better for his son than that? Damn him.* But Kelsey had no reason to think that things should be different — he had no frame of reference, he just knew there was something better than what his father had to offer him.

Brad told him he had picked up too many ideas about love from the music he listened to. Kelsey flicked the volume knob up on the stereo. The fuzzy country song grew to deafening levels even over the roar of the truck's engine. What did Brad know? Why shouldn't he get ideas from songs? Every soul in this town lived the same life, day after day, year after year and, in most cases, generation after generation. Why shouldn't he see what it was like outside the confines of this god-forsaken town? The music that rattled noisily through the speakers seemed to be the only link to something other than this town, these people and Brad.

He stared absently into the never-ending horizon, at the miles and miles of sage brush and low scrubby trees. The monotony of the scenery left his mind a blank canvas with too much room for thinking. Room for thinking about the Desert Rose Angel. *More like a fallen angel*, he thought ruefully. Her painted face and smoky breath hung over him. He could see the premature wrinkles covered over by a layer of beige makeup. Her crimson lips smiled invitingly at him. Her too dark eyes did not. He could feel the naked weight of her pressed against his thighs, her pendulous breasts pressed against his chest, her hands moving lower down his belly.

"Shit," Kelsey muttered under his breath as he slammed on the brakes and grabbed the shifter of the '92. He spun the steering wheel sharply to the right and barely made the turn into his gravel driveway. The nearly bald tires on the truck sent dust spraying behind him as he barreled toward the brown trailer tucked into the sage brush. He came to a skidding stop between Brad's current 1997 Chevy Cheyenne and the rusting bodies of his last two generations of trucks.

The acreage that Brad owned was a graveyard for rusty debris. Car bodies and broken farm equipment lay in ragged pieces over the dusty landscape. Most of them had been there since before Kelsey could remember. As a kid he'd enjoyed exploring the property, finding unique uses for the sharp metal pieces. A loose mower blade turned into a sword to fight aliens. A tractor rake transformed into a multi-toothed monster. He had used the broken chunk of a metal bumper to beat the monster into submission. The mix of junk that littered the ground had provided endless boyhood distraction. That same junk now made him cringe.

Kelsey spit into the dust near the cracked, flat tire of the faded green '81 pickup he parked beside. He kicked a mangled tennis ball into the sage as his feet crunched through the rocky soil toward the trailer. Elsa, the neighbors scrappy border collie mutt that haunted any house that would give her a scrap of food, ran yapping up to him, slobber flying in ribbons around Kelsey's feet. He reached a sun-browned hand down to pat her head as she jumped around his legs, then picked up a broken stick and threw it into the brush. Elsa ran after it, long hairy ears flapping wildly. Kelsey shook his head, a smirk on his lips, and stepped onto the porch. Without thinking he stepped over the boards that were broken through, exposing the dirty depths below. Empty glass Coors bottles rattled together on the loose wood railing of the porch as he slammed the flimsy front door.

The inside of the trailer was permanently dingy. The only light that made it into the living room was filtered through green polyester curtains that hadn't been opened in the last fifteen years. The dim lighting hid the layers of dust that piled up on unused surfaces, old bottles or cans. Standing at the front door, he could see both the living room and the kitchen. A hall stretched to the left down to three bedrooms and a shared bathroom. Some light made it into the kitchen through a sliding glass door. The door was next to what used to be the dining room table but was now a catch-all for mail, trash and miscellaneous small car parts. The hall to the left was dark.

Kelsey hated everything about his dad's house. He rarely spent more time in the communal part of it than it took to walk from the front door or refrigerator to his room. Each time he came home, he mentally counted the amount of money he needed to get out of his dad's house. This day was no different. He started the countdown as soon as the front door slammed, but he was interrupted.

"What the hell are you doing home?" Brad's deep voice drawled from the kitchen where he was leaning his half-naked body against the bar.

"What the fuck do you care?" Kelsey threw his keys on the small table by the door. Brad didn't usually even acknowledge him. He glanced back at his dad. "God, Brad, put some pants on." Kelsey marched into the kitchen, intending to grab a beer before he went to his room.

He was startled as he came around the corner to find a woman in the kitchen, naked except for a thin pair of black underwear that did little to hide the sagging, cellulite-ridden skin of her backside. She was holding a beer and leaning against the opposite side of the counter from Brad, her huge breasts resting solidly on her forearms. She looked boldly at him, clearly used to being seen naked. Kelsey blinked twice, noting that she made no move to interact with him, shook his head and resumed his beer mission.

Opening the yellowed refrigerator, Kelsey glanced inside to find that the woman behind him had taken the last beer. He slammed the door, causing the empties on the counter to rattle. He swung around and looked pointedly at the woman. She continued to stare back at him, little more than amused at his vehemence. He looked her up and down once, then stepped around the bar.

"I didn't know whores made house calls now." Kelsey waited until he was safely out of arms reach before he made the comment. "Service with a smile!" he called loudly as he slammed the bedroom door behind him.

The only place that resembled a refuge in his life was his bedroom. Contrary to the trappings of his upbringing, Kelsey kept his space very well-organized and clean. It was fairly easy considering his lack of possessions, but his bed was always made, clothes were folded neatly in their drawers and the curtains were open and dust-free. He had posters of his favorite cars, Mustangs mostly, neatly pinned to the walls, a remnant of his high-school obsession. His room was the one place that

Brad never came; especially after Kelsey had leveled a punch to Brad's right eye after an unwanted intrusion a year ago. Kelsey had threatened worse. Brad had been too drunk to care.

Kelsey flung himself onto the bed, neatly kicking his shoes under it in one practiced motion. Above him, a buxom woman in a yellow one-piece leaned against a 1981 Red Ford Mustang Cobra. The poster was starting to lose its glossiness but hadn't faded yet. He glanced over the woman's body briefly before focusing his attention on the Cobra.

His mom had owned an '81 Cobra. Brad always said she was a spoiled brat whose daddy got her everything she wanted. Brad sold the car for a paltry amount after his mom died when Kelsey was two years old. When Kelsey was seven, he'd found out that his mom had owned the Cobra, and since then, he'd been fascinated with them. There were other models of the Mustang that far outperformed and outshine the Cobra, but none them captivated him in the same way.

A Cobra had come through the mechanic shop where he worked about three months ago; Kelsey volunteered to change the oil so enthusiastically that the shop owner, Steve, had given him hell for a week. Kelsey didn't care. He washed the car outside and detailed the inside. The owner, a road tripper passing through on the way to Vegas, gave him a pleasantly shocked look and tipped him five dollars. The bill lay in one of his old metal lunch boxes along with a decent number of others in the top drawer of his dresser, waiting for the day Kelsey would get his own Cobra.

While Kelsey was struggling to save up enough to move out and buy a Cobra, his dad had purchased his current truck brand new with the disability check he received every month.

Kelsey resisted the urge to punch the ceiling as he thought about how unfair it was. His dad sat drinking beer with a bad back, driving a new truck, while he worked like a dog, scraping his pennies together.

Kelsey lay in bed and imagined taking the Mustang apart piece by piece and putting it back together again. He heard the front door open, close again and the '97 Cheyenne growl to life. The truck's engine faded down the driveway as it sped onto the highway. Kelsey sighed involuntarily and resettled himself onto his pillow.

He must've fallen asleep for a while because the angle of the light changed through his open window. It had been a deep sleep, especially for the time of day, but something had woken him. He looked around the room and then to the driveway. He saw a small faded red Nissan sedan parked there. Before he could examine it more closely, a faint *tap-tap* on the front door brought him to his feet. He looked to the corner of the room where an old black painted bat leaned against his dresser. They didn't usually get visitors out there, and the thought of greeting one unarmed made him uneasy. He pushed aside his fears. Anyone who drove that little slip of a car probably wasn't a threat.

The young woman was raising her hand to knock on the door again when Kelsey opened it. She jumped a little and took a small step back. He involuntarily smiled when he saw that his assessment of the car had been correct. Definitely not a threat.

"Yes?" he asked the silent woman in front of him. She had regained her composure and was now studying him with what looked like relief. He wondered if she had been worried about knocking, questioning if she was in danger. Apparently she decided that Kelsey wasn't a threat. She smiled slightly, wide pink lips turning up at the corners.

"Is this, um..." She trailed off and glanced down at a rectangular object in her left hand. "...Bradley Campbell's place?"

"Sure is. Why?" He squinted a bit, growing uneasy again.

"Oh. He just left his wallet at the store." She had noticed his change in demeanor; her tone was reassuring. "I think he just dropped it in the parking lot." She held out the dirty-brown wallet to him.

"Okay." Kelsey took it. "Thanks."

Green eyes peered up at him through long brown lashes, calculating. She paused before answering, "Yea. No problem." She lingered for a moment, an unreadable smile playing on her face.

For god's sake, am I supposed to tip the woman? he thought.

Before he could say anything, she raised a hand in farewell, turned and gingerly picked her way across the dilapidated porch and down the steps. Instead of going inside, he watched her get in the Nissan and start it up. She caught him staring at her and leaned forward to grin and wave at him through the windshield. He realized what an idiot he must look like and ducked back in the house, throwing Brad's wallet on the side table next to the truck keys.

He walked into the kitchen, heading for the refrigerator, forgetting that the beer was gone. The refrigerator door closed hard, rattling the contents, just as he heard the front door open. For a moment, he wildly thought that the girl had come back and decided to break in. His heart leapt. He darted his head around the corner and, instead of a slender young woman, saw Brad holding a case of Coors. His stomach dropped at the sight of him. No girl, but at least there was beer again. Brad was looking at the wallet on the side table like it was an alien object.

"How the hell did that get there?"

"Some girl dropped it by just now. Said you left it in the parking lot at the market." Kelsey stood in the kitchen waiting for Brad to bring the beer in.

"Well, that was quick. I went there right before Tina's." He brought the beer in; the bottles rattled as he set the heavy case on the bar. "Was it that pretty-mouthed little brunette?"

"Huh?" Kelsey was trying to tune his dad out but caught his question. "I mean, yes. She had brown hair." Kelsey was surprised to find that he felt a surge of protectiveness. The way Brad said *pretty mouth* made his stomach curdle.

"Everybody says that girl's a whore." Brad flicked the top off a Coors and leaned heavily against the bar. "She's not really my type, but I wouldn't say no to a good fuck." He took a swig of the beer.

Kelsey felt a dangerous flood of heat in his face. He grabbed a cold Coors bottle of his own and clenched it hard.

He isn't worth it, Kelsey thought, trying to calm the rage he felt. After a few deep breaths, a sickening thought passed through his mind. *I probably wouldn't say no either.* This realization was too much. He barged past his father, eyes blurring with anger.

He took the living room in two long strides. He grabbed the keys to his truck, then hurled himself down the steps and into the hot summer sun.

Chapter 3

"I TOLD YOU EARLIER, Kid, I don't have anything for you right now." Steve squinted his bulging eyes and Kelsey imagined a sleepy frog. He snorted. Steve narrowed his eyes farther. "Besides, you know I can't have you work when you've been drinking."

Kelsey ran a hand through his hair, causing the stiff brown locks to stand up at impossible angles. He leaned against the white stucco siding of the shop, heat radiating through his t-shirt and nearly burning his back.

"C'mon, Steve. I need to get more hours in."

"I can't give what I don't have." Steve shook his head and waved toward the office. "Go on inside and sober up."

Kelsey closed his eyes and felt his head spin pleasantly. Air conditioning sounded nice.

"Let me know if somethin' comes in," Kelsey called back to Steve as he aimed his steps toward the office door. Steve watched him from the corner of one round eye, lips squeezed tight.

Kelsey felt thoroughly in control of himself. The ground floated by his feet as he gracefully walked across the black surface of the shop's cement slab. He firmly grabbed the faded brass door knob in one try and smoothly opened it. Without bumping into a wall or piece of furniture, he made his way through the sparsely furnished office. The desk chair gave him more trouble.

Who needs a fucking spinning desk chair anyway? he thought. With a fierce glare, he seized and tamed the spinning beast.

He *needed* Steve to give him work. After being sent home earlier and then dealing with Brad, he had to have some distraction. The beer hadn't been enough. Kelsey had stopped by the Camel Back Market to buy a fifth of tequila, half hoping, half dreading that he would see the pretty girl who had come by the house earlier. No sign of the girl, but after half the bottle of tequila, Kelsey decided that was for the better anyway. He drove to the shop, hoping to find more distraction in the form of cars.

Frustrated, he grabbed the computer mouse and clicked the glowing blue 'e'. The screen was bright for the dark room and he had to squint to find the search bar at the top. Taking a minute to find the right keys on the keyboard he poked at the letters — '1981 Cobra for Sale'.

A number of listings came up; he clicked on one he hadn't seen before. His heart skipped a beat and he leaned forward in his chair. Blinking twice, he refocused his eyes on the details of the newly listed red Mustang Cobra on autotrader.com.

$9,995. Only 4,035 original miles. Saddle leather interior. *Marion, Virginia.*

He blew out a hot breath and slumped back into the chair. There was no way he could get to Virginia. He rubbed rough, oil-stained fingers over his dry eye sockets. The chair bent precariously back under his weight, groaning from the pressure.

The office door opened and closed. The familiar sound of Steve's heavy footsteps scuffed across the short carpet and paused behind him. Metal squealed against metal as the filing cabinet behind him opened, papers rustled and the filing cabinet screeched closed again. Then silence. If he held still enough maybe Steve wouldn't notice him and Kelsey wouldn't need to move or open his eyes in acknowledgment.

"If you'd be willing to wait another year, I know you'd find one close." Steve's burly voice spoke directly over his head, the smell of potato chips and root beer wafting into Kelsey's nose. He opened his eyes, looked up and was greeted with an intimate view of Steve's unshaven Adam's apple. Between the smell and the sight of the greasy old man's bulbous neck, he was acutely aware of the beer and half bottle of tequila that sat gurgling in his gut. The chair snapped back up and he rested on the desk, leaning his forehead against his forearms, taking careful breaths.

He heard Steve snort and head back across the room. "Take your time, Kid," he said before letting the door click closed behind him.

...

The floor stopped rolling. The contents of his gut stopped threatening to eject. He opened his eyes and squinted at the light from the window that was still too bright. Looking around for something to eat, he focused on the metal desk drawer next to his knee. He tugged it open and grabbed a bag of half-eaten Cheetos from inside. The stale cheesy clusters crunched satisfyingly between his teeth. He sighed.

"Help yourself," said a voice from the couch across the room.

A startled jolt made Kelsey pause in his crunching. He hadn't heard Steve re-enter.

Recovering quickly, Kelsey smirked through his chewing. "I will, thanks." Another crunch. "Anything new?"

"Just the usual." Steve readjusted the newspaper he was holding. "People dying, getting married, having babies, killing each other, crashing into things." Kelsey grunted in understanding. Steve peered at Kelsey over the top of the front page. "Anything new with you?"

Kelsey sighed, a small fleck of neon orange flying from his mouth and onto his green t-shirt. He used a long finger to flick it onto the floor. He returned Steve's stare and spoke levelly. "Just the usual."

"Is he bad again?"

"Is he ever good?"

Steve's eyes disappeared behind the newspaper. Kelsey resumed his crunching. He watched Steve fold the paper twice and set it on the plaid fabric of the cushion next to him.

"You know, Kid, I gave you this job because of your daddy. He worked faithfully for me for a lot of years. Since he broke his back in that accident three years ago, I thought I could help your family out by giving you his job." Steve paused and Kelsey made a noise to respond. Steve held up a hand, silencing him. "I know he gets disability. But I still want to help." He gave him a piercing stare and continued, "But I can't help if you won't let me. And I can't let you work here when you show up drunk." The last word hung in the air. Kelsey stared out the window into the amorphous white light.

"How much do you have saved up by now?" Steve asked and settled into the couch cushion, draping his arm over the back.

"Ten." Kelsey's voice was hoarse and quiet.

"And you need twenty?"

Kelsey nodded in the affirmative.

"That's only nine months."

"Only." Kelsey's hooded gaze settled on Steve. Nine months sounded impossible.

"Yes, only. You've made it this far, despite the odds."

The Cheetos bag was empty. Kelsey tossed it lightly on the desk and wiped orange-stained fingers on his pants. The red Cobra was still up on the computer screen. He grabbed the mouse and exited the browser, a bright blue background taking its place.

There was a knock on the door and a well-dressed man in a navy suit opened it. His eyes scanned the room and settled on Kelsey.

"I think something is wrong with my Beamer. Can you take a look?" The man sounded desperate.

Kelsey wondered if the man had ever seen beneath the hood of a car before. After a long look at his crisp white shirt, pristine shiny black shoes and perfectly spiked short black hair, Kelsey decided the man probably hadn't.

Kelsey raised a thick brown eyebrow and waved a hand toward Steve. "Apparently I can't. But he can." Steve shot him a dark look before greeting the man.

"I'll be out in a minute." Steve pushed himself forward on the couch. The man took an anxious look around the office and ran out like a nervous mother attending a sick child. Kelsey laughed, short and deep.

Steve stood and looked out the window, watching the man circle his arctic silver BMW Z3 coupe.

"I know you don't see it, Kid, but you are better than your daddy. You are smart and capable and a good human. Don't make the same mistakes he has." Steve opened the door and stepped outside without waiting for a response.

Ten minutes later, the door to the office crashed open and Kelsey hurtled out, keys in hand. Steve was elbows deep in the BMW. He looked up sharply as Kelsey brushed passed him on the way to his truck.

"Wha—"

"You're wrong," Kelsey growled as he grabbed the metal handle and hoisted himself inside the truck. "I'm just like him." He slammed the door.

Steve shook his head. Kelsey shoved the keys in the ignition, causing the '92 to lurch to life. He pressed the gas pedal to the floor and peeled out onto the highway, dust spraying behind him.

One hour, a six-pack, and the rest of the tequila bottle later, Kelsey's truck sped down the highway, wheels crossing back and forth slowly over the center line. One headlight shone dimly out over the darkened road. The edges of the sky glowed with a blue light, contrasting with the dark horizon. A few stars twinkled faintly overhead. The land was a blur of black until a weak pink line of light encircling a shady sign loomed from the darkness, a focal point for Kelsey's drunken eyes. The lights grew larger and his heartbeat quickened as his destination drew near.

The driveway came sooner than he expected. He pushed hard on the brakes and the '92's tires squealed on the pavement. After putting it in Reverse, he overshot the road and sank the back-left tire into the ditch. He punched the gas. Concentrat-

ing on the dully lit drive, Kelsey got all four tires miraculous-
ly onto the gravel. He barreled down the driveway and double parked in a spray-painted parking space next to two dark
sedans.

His feet crunched through the parking lot and up onto the
wide front porch. A neon blue Budweiser sign glowed brightly from a high window to the left of the door. On the right, a
glowing pink outline of a naked woman in a cowboy hat made
him blink. Kelsey opened and closed the door hard. The hand-
carved Desert Rose Angels sign lightly knocked against the log
cabin exterior of the building.

Two local men, wearing dirty blue jeans and t-shirts, sat at
the bar on the far end of the room. A woman in sky-high shorts
and a plunging black tank top leaned against the backside of
the bar. Long dark hair curled over her shoulder and down her
chest. Her arm was outstretched and her long fingers twirled
through one of the men's unruly hair. She spotted Kelsey as he
came in and winked at him. In a quick movement she jumped
onto the bar, swung her legs over the smooth dark wood and
straddled the man with unruly hair, knees pressed to his shoulders. He put his hands on her waist, pulling her briefly onto his
lap. The two stood up and headed through a door to the right
side of the bar.

The pair passed another woman on her way into the room.
This one was shorter and blond with breasts that wobbled precariously over the top of her skin-tight red dress.

Charity.

"Kelsey. Baby." Charity ignored the second man sitting at
the bar and embraced Kelsey, pulling him close by the small of
his back and kissing his mouth lightly.

"How'r you, Char?"

Her dark painted eyes flashed to his face. She disguised her startlement at his state of intoxication by burying her lips into his neck.

"I'm so good now that you're here, Baby." She spoke into his neck, lips lightly brushing over the rough stubble of his chin. "How are you doing?" Drawing on hard-won acting skills, she kept the concern out of her voice.

Kelsey grunted. "Just now, Char, I need t'sit."

She grabbed his hand and led him to a wood bar stool next to a dancing pole at the end of the bar. Using the pole and Charity's shoulder for support, he sat heavily onto the stool.

Charity crossed to the opposite side of the bar, took a long look at Kelsey, and poured him a glass of water. She set it carefully down in front of him and he stared at it for a long minute before grabbing the water. It ran down his chin as he drank deeply. He finished it off and Charity reached across to wipe the trickle from his face.

The pale tops of her breasts hung just inches from his face. Deep in his drunkenness and mesmerized by the soft swellings, he reached across the bar and grabbed her chest. Charity squeaked but didn't move. She looked from his hand to his face and smiled coyly.

"Now, Kelsey, you know better than that!" Her tone was indignant, her eyes amused. She softly took his hand off her chest and let it fall to the bar top.

The man sitting two stools down had been watching with some interest, but jumped to his feet when a tall woman with jet black hair and glowing brown skin entered the room from the side bar. Her dark lips spread into an inviting smile, chocolate eyes locked on his face.

"I'm ready for you, Ted." Her voice hummed like a swarm of bees and flowed like honey.

The man, apparently named Ted, was visibly vibrating as he followed her through the doorway, leaving Charity and Kelsey alone.

Sex hung in the air as thick as a fog bank around them. Faint country music floated from a portable radio behind the bar. Charity's brown eyes burned flaming holes into his. She bit one full pink lower lip, considering him for a minute.

"Do you want a drink or..." Her girlish voice trailed off as she glanced toward the doorway.

Kelsey's hooded eyes looked slowly toward the door and back to the glass that had held his water. Realizing his mouth was open, he closed it and looked up. Charity was watching him.

"C'mon, Baby. You need it. And so do I." She looked down at her chest and brought her hand up to the side of her breast. Kelsey made an indistinct sound of consent. Feeling unsteady, he waited until she came around the bar to grab his hand and lead him through the doorway.

Kelsey watched his feet as he put one black booted foot in front of the other, following her red pumps down the hall across paisley carpet. Somewhere along the way, Kelsey lost track of which shoe was his. Each one blended with the other, black and red swirling together with purple paisley. The earth tilted up and gravity melted away. The dark opening to the room yawned in front of him, drawing him into a new gravitational pull. The door clicked closed behind him and his universe plunged into darkness.

...

The first thing he became aware of was that his vision alternated between glowing red and black; the second was that he was naked; the third was that he was not alone. Being hungover was a familiar feeling and he knew it was not a good idea to sit up quickly. So he kept his eyes closed until he made sense of at least part of his surroundings.

He concentrated on figuring out who was with him. Chancing a small movement of his hand, he found it was resting on a naked butt — soft, yet firm, and hairless. A woman. That explained why he was naked too. He took a deep breath; the pieces were coming together.

The deep breath triggered a wave of nausea. He reflexively leaned over the side of the bed, groping for something to vomit into. Though the room was mostly dark, he managed to grab a well-placed trash can. He emptied his stomach into it, vaguely recognizing that, until now, a used condom was the trash receptacles only contents. After a minute of violent heaving, he was satisfied with the emptiness of his stomach. He wiped his hand across his mouth. Regaining his breath, he flopped back onto the bed, eyes closed, head pounding.

As his breathing normalized, the pounding in his head slowed and blurred into a dull ache. The woman next to him stirred and rested a hand lightly on his bare chest.

It couldn't be her, could it? he thought and his heartbeat quickened, causing a swell of nausea again. Putting his thoughts on hold until he mastered his innards, he took a steadying breath. The nausea was graciously fleeting.

After a few more moments his memories started to return. He remembered driving for a half hour after leaving Steve's shop. He remembered pulling into a rural gas station and cutting the engine after the sun started to sink low in the sky.

Her face had haunted him as he sat in the gas station parking lot. The girl who'd stopped by the house had had a beautiful, playful, innocent face. He smiled picturing it. But Brad's words, and his own, threatened to drive Kelsey over the brink.

Everybody says that girl's a whore...

...I probably wouldn't say no either.

After buying a six-pack of Coors at the gas station, he sat in his truck, finished the bottle of tequila and drank the six-pack while he watched the sun sink lower and finally blink below the horizon.

Most days, he was able to ignore the reality that he was so much like Brad. He threw himself into work and dreamed of the day when he could get away. When work wasn't distracting enough, drinking helped him forget their similarities. And when drinking didn't suffice, he would drive to the brothel. The girls worked every time.

As he had sat in the truck, he wondered if the girl who came by the house really was a prostitute. That would be a comfort. Then he wouldn't have to feel ashamed of his feelings toward her. Maybe he could even find her.

Occupied by his thoughts, he hadn't realized how drunk he was until he'd stepped out of the truck to take a pee. The alcohol fog had crashed through his brain like a tidal wave. He'd held the side of his truck to stabilize himself and then pulled his bulk unsteadily back into the truck and watched as the last pink streaks disappeared from the sky.

The same pink as the girl's lips.

He had grabbed the keys hanging in the ignition and started the truck.

The woman at his side stirred again, running her fingers through the bit of hair in the middle of his chest and sighing contentedly. Her breath tickled his shoulder. The tickle made his skin crawl as he tried to recall if he had found the girl from earlier and ended up in bed with her. He tried to remember, but failed.

The back of his eyelids still flashed from red to black, disorienting him. He wondered if it was some kind of strobe light. He didn't want to look, fearing he would see the beautiful girl that he had set out to find. After a minute though, his heart started to race, the nausea flared again and he decided to look.

He cracked one eye open. Through his lashes he saw a mess of blond hair resting on the pillow at his shoulder. The girl who came to the house had had brown hair.

Not her. He let his eye close again. He softly let his breath out. *Not her.*

A red flash caused his eyes to blink open again, looking for the source of the annoyance. A small fan in the corner of the room blew a heavy dark curtain over the window. Bright daylight intermittently shone from behind.

Shit, Kelsey thought, accompanied by an audible groan. *It's morning.*

He pushed himself carefully up to rest his back on the upholstered headboard, ignoring the pounding in his skull. The blond head at his thigh turned up to reveal a sleepy painted face.

Charity.

"Char, why'd you let me stay here? You know I can't afford all night." Kelsey rubbed a hand over his eyes.

She moved her hand slowly up his inner thigh. He pushed it gently but firmly away.

"I can't pay you back," Kelsey said, stressing his seriousness.

She rested her head on his naked belly. "I know, Baby. But I didn't want to drag your passed-out ass out of here last night." She giggled into his belly button, causing the hair on his arms to raise. "Besides, I'll give you a discount for last night. You were fun." She began to kiss the top of his thigh.

"Stop, Char." Kelsey put a hand on her head to stop her efforts. "I don't want to get in deeper than I already am." She looked up at him, lower red lip pushed out. "I appreciate the discount though." She smiled and raised herself up, resting her head on his shoulder and draping her naked body against his side.

"Are you sure you don't want to fuck this morning?" she asked sweetly.

"Yes, I'm sure. I'm especially sure you don't want me to throw up in here again."

She made a pouty sound and swung her legs off the bed. Standing up, she grabbed the red dress that lay discarded in a heap on the nightstand. She pulled it over her head and tugged it down her curvy body. She flipped the lamp on. Kelsey blinked.

"Just take twenty bucks off," she said as she sat back down on the bed to strap on her red pumps.

Kelsey scanned the floor for his pants. He didn't have to reach far. He pulled his wallet out and handed her a stack of twenties. He briefly wondered if he would stop coming here if he stopped carrying cash.

"Thanks, Baby. Take your time getting out of here. I'll see you next time, hm?" She smiled pleasantly and stood up.

Kelsey smiled back distractedly, thinking. She moved toward the doorway. "Hey, Char. Do you have a new girl working here?" He paused and fumbled for words. "Darkish brown hair, green eyes, my age, maybe?"

Charity raised her eyebrows a bit and leaned against the doorframe. "No, Baby. You know all of us."

Kelsey waved her off. "Never mind then. Thanks again."

Charity blew him a kiss and walked out, leaving Kelsey alone. Again.

Chapter 4

A TINY BELL JINGLED just inches over his head as he pushed the worn wood handle on the heavy swinging door. A cool whoosh of air carried the thick smell of cigarettes and stale alcohol from inside the store. Inside, it was surprisingly light for such a small building. The ceiling was high with a row of windows on the wall under it that were long overdue for a washing. The ancient-looking wood floor groaned as he stepped inside, letting the door swing closed behind him. A few ceiling fans slightly lifted the hair on his head as he scanned the one-room store for her brown locks.

This was the third time in as many days that he had come to the Camel Back Market to look for the girl who had preoccupied his thoughts. Each afternoon he had to come up with some excuse to be there, usually beer, but there had been no sign of the girl. This time, he came in the morning, thinking that it was the only time he hadn't tried. And if she wasn't there this time, he was done looking; done with the ridiculous fascination.

He wasn't even sure why he was so obsessed with her. Maybe it was the mystery, the unknown of a new face. Maybe it was the way she'd smiled when she'd left his house that day. And maybe, to his mortification, it was that he wanted to see whether she was a whore. Whatever the reason, here he was again.

Kelsey spotted her right away. She was behind the counter, smiling slightly at the wrinkled man who was buying cigarettes, beer and a half gallon of milk. She nodded and waved as the stooped man grabbed his purchases and brushed past Kelsey, the thick scent of motor oil and tobacco following him out of the store. Her eyes followed the man and met Kelsey's gaze. She smiled widely and lifted a hand in greeting. He did the same, feeling like a fool.

His only reason for being here was to see her, but he thought he'd better not act like it. He was passably hungry, so he went for the plastic box full of jerky sticks on the far side of the counter. As he busied himself with the jerky, he watched her covertly. She was helping another customer, the same small smile playing at the corner of her mouth. Her long, straight brown hair fell in a curtain around her face as she leaned forward to put the money in the cash register. The move gave him a good view of her backside. As he was absently appreciating the sight, she turned and caught his stare. She frowned at him and went back to helping her customer. Kelsey nearly dropped the jerky stick in his haste to look away. He turned on his boot and headed for the back of the store.

Better get this over with, he thought.

He took a deep breath, held his jerky and 22 oz Coca-Cola in one hand, and walked back to the front of the store, boots clopping on the hardwood floor. He kept his gaze down, only looking up when he reached the counter. A pair of striking green eyes met his, alight with amusement. It brought an unexpected smile from him, followed by a nervous grunt that was meant to be a greeting.

"Hey," she said, still smiling like a cat that caught a bird. She reached forward to take his Coke.

Kelsey found he had to clear his throat. "Look, I'm sorry about..." Mortifying himself, he watched his hand move vaguely in the direction of her backside.

"Forget about it," she interrupted him, placing his Coke back on the counter. She waved his apology off with a graceful fair hand.

"It's just, you looked upset," he blurted out.

Shut up, Dumbass! he thought. *Just leave it.*

She giggled. "Well, I'm used to it around here. But that doesn't mean I like it." Kelsey looked down in embarrassment. "Like I said though, I'm used to it. I'm the only thing on two legs with boobs most of these men have seen all day." She laughed again, but without humor. "Jeannie gets it too."

Kelsey looked up to see her nodding toward a short, friendly looking woman walking in from the back room carrying a double stack of paper cups that was threatening to topple over. The woman, Jeannie, gave him a look that severely questioned his intentions before bustling behind the counter. She shoved the cups into their place under the counter, her expansive bottom swaying from side to side as she maneuvered them around.

"Two-nineteen for you today." His head popped up from watching Jeannie and green eyes met his again.

"Oh, uh, yea." He handed her a couple dollar bills and loose change. "Thank you." He nodded toward her and grabbed his things.

"Jordyn, it's your break, Hon." Jeannie's gravelly voice came from below the counter. "I'll take the next 15 minutes." Jeannie stood up and smiled at her coworker, a thousand wrinkles fanning around her eyes.

Jordyn, huh? Pretty name. Kelsey turned from the counter to head out the door, the thrill of discovery making his steps light.

"Oh, thanks!" Jordyn replied. He saw her pull the strings on her dark green apron until it popped free and she threw it under the counter. Realizing he couldn't watch her all day, he reluctantly let the door swing behind him.

The desert heat hit him as his feet crunched across the sandy gravel outside the market. Twisting the cap from his Coke, he took a long cold drink before getting in his truck.

"Hey!" a woman's voice called in his direction. He turned to see Jordyn leaning against the shady side wall of the market, looking at him. He motioned toward himself.

She talking to me? he wondered briefly. *Of course she is, you idiot. There's no one else here.* The realization gave him another small thrill and he tentatively stepped her way.

"Can I have one?" She pointed toward his chest.

"A Coke?" he asked stupidly.

She laughed. "No, you have cigarettes."

"Oh yea, for sure!" He smiled and fumbled with the box in his pocket.

"Slow down there, Tiger," she said. "I'm not in a rush."

He handed her a cigarette and flicked his lighter on with a practiced hand. She leaned forward and lit up. Watching her perfectly pink lips around the cigarette distracted him and he forgot to close the lighter. She raised an eyebrow and smirked.

"You going to have a smoke too?" she asked.

"Oh yea, for sure!" he replied, flustered.

As he lit his cigarette, he watched her take a long inhale, close her eyes and lean against the peeling green paint of the wall.

"I haven't smoked in what feels like ages!" she said as she smiled contentedly at him. "Thank you." She raised the hand holding the cigarette in salute. He nodded, not sure what to say. Instead, he leaned against the wall next to her, keeping a respectful distance.

"What's your name?" she asked.

"Kelsey." His voice came out husky with the smoke. "And you're Jordyn?" She nodded.

"Kelsey." She paused. "Isn't that a girl's name?"

"Isn't Jordyn a boy's name?" he asked in defense.

She looked at him in surprise before they both started laughing. It was a minute before they caught their breathes.

"Well, Kelsey, it's nice to meet you." She leaned her head back on the wall.

"Why is it that I've not met you before? You go to high school around here?" Kelsey asked.

"I usually work the morning shift at the store and take care of my sister in the afternoon. If you don't come in early to the store, you don't see me." She took another pull on the cigarette, finishing it. "I didn't go to the high school. I was home-schooled." Her light tone dropped a little at this.

"Homeschooled. Did you like it?" *Am I being too nosey?* he wondered. He couldn't help it. He had to know this girl.

"Mmm, no." She glanced sideways at him and tapped the cigarette with her finger, knocking grey dust into the air. "But my sister has Down syndrome, so I need to be around to take care of her."

"Why don't your parents take care of her?" he asked automatically.

She swung her shoulder around, turning her whole body toward him and squinted her eyes. "Kelsey. You have lots of questions, don't you?" He looked at the toe on his boot, realizing how rude he had been.

"Sorry," he muttered.

"No, no. It's okay," she said. "Actually, it's kind of refreshing." She bent and rubbed the cigarette into the gravel.

"You don't have to answer."

"It's alright." She stood up. "My dad left when my mom had my sister. My mom is worthless." She said this matter-of-factly. Kelsey nodded, understanding too clearly.

They looked at each other in silence before Jordyn extended her hand.

"Nice to meet you, Kelsey." He transferred his half-smoked cigarette into his left hand and grasped her outstretched one. It fit neatly into his as he gently shook it.

"My pleasure, Darlin'."

Darlin'?! He was horrified. *Get it together, man!*

She giggled a bit. "Darlin'? Are you a cowboy or somethin'?" Not waiting for his response, she gave his hand a small squeeze and let go. "I like it." In one fluid movement, she turned on one heel and headed toward the front door of the store.

"I get off at noon tomorrow." She looked back at him, a question in her eyes.

"That's my lunch," Kelsey replied to her unspoken request.

Her answering smile hit him square in the chest. It took a few minutes before his legs were able to carry him back to his truck.

...

"You've been too chatty today." Steve's voice came from under a gold Buick LeSabre that was perched six feet in the air on a car lift.

"I didn't realize that was a crime," Kelsey answered, grabbing his keys from among the miscellaneous car parts on the workshop's metal counter.

"It's not. Just unusual for you." The sound of an air wrench echoed through the shop's rafters.

"Well, I'll work on it," Kelsey said wryly.

"Where are you going?"

"Just grabbing lunch. I'll be back before the 1:30 comes in."

"You going to the market? Pick me up a Mountain Dew. There's a five on the counter."

"Alright..." Kelsey trailed off and peered at Steve under the LeSabre. The fabric of Steve's grey t-shirt was soaked through in the armpits as he struggled with the innards of the Buick. "How did you know I was going to the market?"

"I didn't."

Kelsey grunted and walked back to the counter. He grabbed the five-dollar bill and shoved it in his pocket. "Back in a few."

"Enjoy your lunch." Steve peaked from around his sweaty arm and grinned.

Kelsey shook his head and headed for the truck.

...

She was standing next to the faded red Nissan she had driven to his house earlier that week. She wore the same clothes that she was wearing when he shared a cigarette with her the day before: a pair of cutoff blue jeans, black and white sneakers and a black t-shirt. He couldn't help the smile that pulled at the corners of his mouth. Seeing her there, waiting for him, gave him the same kind of thrill he had paid good money for in the past. She saw his smile and returned it, ducking her head shyly and pushing a strand of hair behind her ear.

Before he cut the engine, she held up her hand in a stopping motion. He frowned and watched as she walked to the passenger side of his truck, opened the door and hopped in.

"Hey," she said brightly as she settled herself on his bench seat.

"Uh, hey," he said, unsure of himself.

"I picked up an afternoon shift at the market today. But I need to run home during my lunch and check on my sister. Can you give me a ride?"

"Oh yea, sure." He was thrilled to have her in his truck, but uncertainty crept into his voice.

She ignored his tone and buckled the seat belt around her. "Great, thanks!"

He put the truck into gear. "Where are we goin'?"

"Turn right. I'm about ten miles south of town." She motioned out the window.

"You got it." He pulled out of the gravel parking lot.

They sat in silence for a moment. Kelsey realized he had just met this girl and knew little about who she was. He considered what he did know. She was a beautiful woman: long legs, fair skin, dark brunette hair, striking green eyes and perfect full lips. So beautiful, he had a hard time concentrating on the pavement. Oblivious to his thoughts, she sat with her elbow rested against the truck door, playing with a strand of hair.

Kelsey began to say "So—" just as she said, "Hey, thanks—" They laughed at the awkward interruption. Kelsey motioned for her to talk.

"I just wanted to say thanks for driving me. I guess I shouldn't have asked. You don't really know me and I don't know you." She paused, thoughtful, a small frown furrowing her brow.

"I was just thinking the same thing." He smiled in what he hoped was a reassuring way. "You can trust me though."

She looked at him then, serious. "Yea. I mean, I thought so." She looked out the side window.

"Isn't it crazy we can live in such a small town and never have met?" Kelsey was anxious to find out more about her.

She glanced back at him; her thoughtfulness replaced with a relaxed smile. "I know. Crazy! I was pretty isolated growing up though."

"Me too." Now it was his turn to be serious.

"Really?" She sounded surprised.

Kelsey nodded. "Really."

"You seem like what I would picture as the popular kid in school. Handsome football player, cheerleaders hanging on your arm, all that."

Kelsey laughed. "I've been called a bad kid, troubled, disadvantaged and deviant, but never popular. That's would be a first."

A puzzled frown crossed her face. "I guess my read on people is off then. Blame it on the homeschooling." She laughed sardonically.

"What about you? You don't seem like a homeschooler." Kelsey looked pointedly at her as long as he dared while driving. "Isn't homeschooling for nerdy, Bible-thumping conservative families?"

"Ha! No Bible-thumping, nerdy, conservative family here! Apparently homeschooling is also for families with a tweaker mom, a disabled daughter and a skinny white girl with no daddy." She smiled sideways at him and shrugged. "Sorry. That got depressing."

Kelsey nodded, trying to match her mood, which appeared to be mostly light-hearted.

"You make the best of it though, you know?" she said.

"Yea. I do know."

"So, what's your story then, Kelsey?"

"Nothing exciting. My dad is an out of work alcoholic. My mom died when I was two. I have a sister but she lives with her mom in Sacramento. I've never left Nevada, never played sports, never done anything really."

Jordyn laughed. "Wow. A deviant and a homeschooler. Don't we make quite the pair."

In other circumstances, Kelsey would have cuffed anyone who dared laughed at him, and had in the past. But he wasn't offended by Jordyn's laughter. He sensed she understood somehow. He found himself smiling with her.

"Turn right up here, at the next phone pole."

Kelsey turned the '92 down a dirt road leading to a cluster of six trailers at a dead end. Jordyn directed him to a single wide light blue trailer, the last one on the left. He parked in the small driveway and Jordyn hopped out of the truck, slamming the door behind her.

The trailer was surprisingly well-kept considering the state of the other trailers they passed. No piles of garbage or rusty metal littered the yard. Someone had shoved fake flowers into the brick-lined flower beds out front. A short plastic white picket fence surrounded the driveway. A small, clean-swept porch jutted out from the front of the trailer.

Jordyn bounded up the few steps to the front door and motioned him up. He followed, feeling awkward about being at the home of a woman he'd just met.

"Come on in."

Taking a deep breath, Kelsey followed her.

The interior of the trailer was as clean as the outside. A cool breeze, provided by a small window air-conditioning unit, flowed out of the door as they entered. More fake flowers stood in a vase on the coffee table. A television squawked loudly beyond the coffee table.

As they walked in, a short girl who was sitting on one of the faded blue couches in front of the television stood up and turned around. A huge smile overcame her round face, causing her eyes to turn into half-moons. She ran around the couch and grabbed Jordyn in a giant embrace, holding her tight. Jordyn held her just as tightly, resting her cheek on the girl's head. Their hair blended together, an exact match.

"Hi, Lizzie Girl. How was your morning?" Jordyn pulled back but kept her hands on her shoulders.

"Good. How was your morning?" Lizzie replied, continuing to smile at Jordyn.

"Busy, but good. Where's Mama?" Jordyn glanced around the room that served as a living room and kitchen.

"Sleeping," Lizzie said simply. She glanced at Kelsey, suddenly aware of his presence. A look of unsure wariness overcame her face. "Is that guy checking on us?"

Jordyn cupped Lizzie's face with her hand. "No, Honey. This is my friend. His name is Kelsey." Jordyn turned to Kelsey. "Kelsey, this is my sister, Lizzie." She smiled, obviously completely smitten with her sister.

"Hi, Kelsey." Lizzie smiled faintly while timidly waving one of her hands.

"Hi, Lizzie." Kelsey held his hand out. Lizzie slowly reached out her own. His encompassed hers and he gently shook it. She gave him a shy smile.

Jordyn walked into the kitchen and Kelsey watched as Lizzie followed her and Jordyn pulled out bread, peanut butter and jam from the cupboard. Lizzie watched her sister with wide-eyed attention. Kelsey estimated that Lizzie was in her mid to late teens, probably a few years younger than her sister. She had a sweet innocent face with wide brown eyes. She was dressed simply in a pair of khaki shorts and a light blue t-shirt. Her hair was straight with short bangs.

"Do you want one?" Jordyn motioned with a butter knife to the ingredients laid out on the counter.

"Sure, if it's not too much trouble." Kelsey was touched by her simple offer. He didn't remember the last time anyone had made him food.

"Did Mama get any of your school done today?" Jordyn said as she picked up a piece of bread and smeared jam over it.

"No," Lizzie replied, licking her lips.

Jordyn sighed. "Alright, we'll have to finish it up this weekend. I picked up an extra shift at work this afternoon."

"Okay. Will you be gone tonight too?" Lizzie asked.

Jordyn's eyes flicked to Kelsey's face briefly before answering. "No. I'll be home tonight. I'm going to have Jeannie check in on you later this afternoon though, okay?"

Lizzie didn't reply. She was absorbed in examining the peanut butter and jam sandwich. Kelsey smiled at Lizzie. She smiled back, apparently comfortable with his presence now.

"Here you go." Jordyn handed him a sandwich wrapped in a paper towel. He took it gratefully.

They ate in silence, Jordyn and Kelsey exchanging amused glances as they watched Lizzie meticulously nibble the crust.

When they finished, Jordyn excused herself and headed down the hall. Kelsey took the opportunity to look around the space. He wandered into the living area. It was sparsely furnished with two small couches and a coffee table. In addition to the vase of silk flowers sitting on the table, there were a few loose pieces of unopened mail addressed to Cynthia Carver. The television, currently playing the Discovery Channel, sat on a low bookshelf. He bent over to examine the books, which were a mixture of romance novels, textbooks and school workbooks.

"Those are my school books," Lizzie said proudly from behind him.

"Does your sister teach you school?" He looked back at Lizzie.

"Yes." Lizzie nodded enthusiastically, her face smeared with peanut butter. "I'm in the eleventh grade."

"Wow. Your sister takes good care of you."

"Yes, she does. She buys me nice things." Lizzie pulled at her blue shirt, indicating that it was one of the nice things.

"I have a sister too," Kelsey said.

"Does she buy you nice things?"

"No, but she is a great sister. I love her a lot." Kelsey was surprised at the tenderness this girl pulled from him. He never spoke that way about anybody, ever.

"Do you want me to sing you a song?" Lizzie asked suddenly.

Kelsey opened his mouth, not sure what to say. "Uh—" he began.

"Maybe next time," Jordyn spoke from the entrance to the hallway. She was leaning against the corner, watching them with a sweet smile. "Kelsey and I need to get back to work."

"Okay. I will miss you," Lizzie said.

"You know I miss you too." Jordyn walked to the kitchen sink and grabbed a wash cloth. She tenderly wiped the remains of the sandwich off Lizzie's face. Lizzie stood obediently still.

"Will you sing me a song next time?" Kelsey asked as Lizzie used her forearm to wipe the moisture from her face.

"Yes!" she replied.

"Alright, I'll see you tonight. Wake Mama up if you need anything." Jordyn kissed the top of Lizzie's head. Lizzie pushed out her lips and waited. Jordyn leaned forward and gave her another kiss. "Love you."

"Love you too." Lizzie walked over to the couch and sat down, resuming her television show about elephants.

Kelsey looked at Jordyn. Their eyes met and she nodded, motioning for the door.

"She'll be okay," Jordyn said after they sat down in the truck. "I could never leave when she was younger, but she has a bit more independence now. My mom will usually help if she really needs something, and I have Jeannie check in when I can't be there."

"She seems really sweet," Kelsey said as he started the engine.

"She is. She can be maddening, but I like taking care of her. She needs me." Jordyn looked out her window at the blue trailer as they pulled out of the driveway. "Thanks again for coming with me."

"Sure, no problem. Thanks for the sandwich."

"No problem." Jordyn sighed contentedly and smiled at him.

"Is your last name Carver?" Kelsey asked, remembering the unopened mail on the coffee table.

"Yes, sir," she replied. "My mom is Cynthia but everybody calls her Cindy. My sister is Elizabeth but I've always called her Lizzie."

"I like it," he said.

"Yea, it fits her."

"Do you want a smoke?" Kelsey patted his pocket.

"Oh, no, thanks though. Actually, I quit a couple weeks ago. It was a bitch. I, uh, actually just wanted an excuse to talk to you yesterday." She smiled shyly into her lap. Kelsey beamed.

"Really?" he asked, just to make sure he'd heard her right.

"Really," she replied. "But go ahead and have one if you want. I don't mind."

"That's alright," Kelsey said, dismissing the idea. He glanced over at her, giddy with the knowledge that this beautiful woman had wanted to meet him as much as he'd wanted to meet her.

She seemed content to end that conversation so he decided to change the subject. "Do you pick up a lot of night shifts?" Jordyn looked up from her lap. Kelsey continued, "It's only, Lizzie asked if you were going to be gone tonight too. So I thought..."

Jordyn turned to him with a grin. "You sure talk a lot for a bad boy. Aren't you supposed to be silently brooding over a motorcycle or something?"

Kelsey was surprised. Her tease hadn't pushed his buttons. Instead, he laughed with her again.

"But seriously though," Jordyn continued. "You were so sweet to my sister. Not everybody is like that. I just don't see the bad boy in you."

"Yet," Kelsey said, gloomily.

"Yet," she repeated. "Does that mean we will see each other again?" Her tone was hopeful. His heart skipped a happy beat.

"I'd like to," he replied seriously.

"I'd like that too."

They sat in pleasant silence until Kelsey pulled into the Camel Back Market parking lot. He didn't turn the truck off, hoping she wouldn't go quickly. Her head was down, focused on her lap. She looked up. The sun shone with its full intensity outside the truck, illuminating the loose hairs around her head in iridescent copper. Their eyes met and held, communicating more in one look than if they had spoken a thousand words. After what felt like forever, they broke their gaze.

He opened his mouth, but she interrupted him quietly, "I have to work and get caught up on Lizzie's school this weekend. But do you want to meet here again on Monday?" She fumbled with her words a bit, then ducked her head down and back up to meet his eyes again, waiting for an answer.

"There's nothing I'd enjoy more, Darlin.'" Kelsey hoped he sounded as sincere as he felt.

Luminescent light flooded her eyes and face. All her teeth shone in her wide smile. She nodded. "Darlin,'" she repeated. "I still like it."

They sat in silence again, both unsure of how to say good-bye. She was the one to break the quiet. With a mischievous smirk and an outstretched hand, she said, "Nice to meet you again, Kelsey Campbell."

He returned the look and reached his left hand around to grasp hers. It was soft and warm and still fit perfectly into his. "Nice to meet you again as well... Darlin.'" He squeezed her hand lightly.

She winked, opened the truck door and jumped out. With a wave, she was gone, slamming the door behind her. He watched her walk back into the market, feeling a small part of himself walk through the door with her.

It wasn't until he pulled into the shop's parking lot that he realized he'd completely forgotten Steve's Mountain Dew.

Chapter 5

EVEN THOUGH THEY HAD made plans for him to visit her at the market on Monday, Kelsey went to the Camel Back Market every day for the next three mornings instead. She was there each time and always appeared delighted to see him. On the third morning, after Kelsey purchased yet another Mountain Dew for Steve, she gave him her phone number with a shy smile very unlike any he'd seen from her before.

It took another three days for Kelsey to call. He had finally drudged up the courage to ask her on a real date. He decided to call in the evening when she was sure to be at home.

He thought he could take her to the Mexican restaurant in town. Then, if she was up for it, he could show her around the shop. Steve okayed this plan with the strong stipulation that there would be no 'funny business' in the client's cars or in his office. Kelsey agreed, though was secretly disappointed he had done so. After briefly considering not calling her, desire prevailed. He held the cell phone close to his ear while it rang, sweat beading between his skin and the plastic casing.

"Hullo," a raspy woman's voice answered.

Kelsey took a quick inhale of breath. This was not the voice he'd expected.

"Hullo?" the woman said again. When Kelsey did not answer she said angrily, "Look, if this is the fucking state calling again, I'm going to fucking..."

"No—" Kelsey interrupted her, finally finding his voice. "No... I'm sorry. I was just looking for Jordyn. I, uh, must have the wrong number."

"Jordyn?" the woman spoke slowly. "What do you want with her?"

"She, ah, gave me this number. I..." Kelsey trailed off. He couldn't tell this woman that he'd been calling to ask Jordyn on a date.

"Well, she's out." The woman suddenly sounded very tired. He heard jostling on the other end of the line as the woman spoke again, this time obviously irritated. "Lizzie, no. Just go back to your fucking bed. God—" The line cut off and Kelsey's phone blinked black.

He stared at it in his hand. He must have just spoken with Jordyn's mama.

Not wanting to repeat the previous night's phone conversation, Kelsey visited the market again the next morning. Jordyn was there and Kelsey briefly wondered if she ever took a day off. She looked tired as he entered the market, bells jingling overhead. When she recognized him, she gave him half a smile as she finished putting a box of Rice Krispies on one of the shelves in front of her. He smiled back and walked down the aisle. Before he could speak, she held up her hand.

"I know you called last night," she said, her voice sounded tired. "I'm sorry you had to talk to her." Jordyn grimaced.

Kelsey opened his mouth to protest but she held up her hand again and spoke. "Lizzie told me someone called for me and that Mama answered. I'm sorry."

"It's really no big deal." Kelsey spoke before she had a chance to talk. "Look, I'm used to being embarrassed by parents, okay?" When she didn't speak, he continued, "Brad Campbell is my dad. I don't know if you know him, but ask anybody around. He's the worst son of a bitch. So, don't worry about it." His voice was soft and persuasive.

She looked into his face, checking for sincerity. He gave her a smile that he hoped was reassuring.

"Okay," she said finally and put the last box of cereal on the shelf. "I'm still sorry though."

Kelsey shrugged.

"What are you here for today?" Her voice lightened, though he still saw the lines of fatigue around her eyes. "Are you getting another Mountain Dew?" She looked at him playfully from the corners of her eyes.

Kelsey snorted and shrugged again. He ran a hand through his hair and shifted his weight from left to right.

Moving suddenly, she turned her body to face him. Her chest rose as she took a deep breath. Her fingers flexed next to her thighs. Her eyes flickered with light and searched his face. "Just why are you here?" Her voice was shockingly forceful. This was a challenge, not a question.

"I want to ask you on a date," Kelsey blurted, confused by her sudden change of mood. Before he had a chance to regret his sudden outburst, a wide smile transformed her face. He found himself smiling back. She bit her lip and ducked her head, still smirking.

"I mean... Well... That wasn't how I planned on asking you," Kelsey said more slowly this time. She looked back at him without speaking, eyes shining. After a long moment, Kelsey shifted himself again. "Well? Would you—"

"Yes," she interrupted him. "Yes, I would like to go on a date with you, Kelsey Campbell." She smiled while shyly looking at him through her lowered lashes.

A fiery burst of happiness started at the base of his lungs and filled him like a hot air balloon. Forgetting they were in public and that she was at work, he reached his hand out, grasped hers and pulled her to him in an embrace. Her head rested lightly on his chest. He inhaled deeply and drew the scent of her hair into his lungs. As he exhaled, he heard a sound behind him.

"I have put up with you coming in here and flirting with my cashier, but I'll be damned if I'm going to let you molest her right in front of my eyes."

Jordyn quickly pulled away from Kelsey and they both moved to face a very red-faced Jeannie, brandishing a broom like a sword at Kelsey. Kelsey stood still, shocked by the fierce little woman in front of him. Jordyn stifled a burst of laughter. She rearranged her expression to one of solemnity, and spoke.

"Jeannie. It's okay." Jordyn held out a hand toward the broom that waved menacingly in Kelsey's stunned face. Jeannie chanced a glance at Jordyn and her fierce expression flickered.

"Really, Jeannie. He's just asked me out on a date," Jordyn continued. Jeannie resumed her vicious glare. "I said yes, Jeannie. I want to go out with him." Jeannie looked fully at Jordyn now with a strange expression.

"This boy?" Jeannie asked, sounding a bit strangled. She poked Kelsey in the chest with the broom. The straw bristles poked through his shirt, pricking him. "This boy?"

"Yes! I don't see anyone else in here!" Jordyn's voice raised a pitch and she threw up her hands.

Jeannie lowered her voice and spoke conspiratorially to Jordyn as if Kelsey couldn't hear. "Don't you know about this boy? Jordyn, please."

Jordyn's eyes sparked. She straightened her back and pushed out her chest. Speaking in full volume she said, "I know all I need to know about this man, Jeannie. And I will be going out on a date with him."

Jeannie's eyes flicked to Kelsey and appraised him quickly. Apparently displeased, she looked back at Jordyn and gave her a pleading look. Jordyn looked directly into Kelsey's eyes.

"I have tomorrow afternoon off, after 3:00. Does that work?" Jordyn's voice was a little louder than it needed to be.

"Uh, yea. I will pick you up from your house then," Kelsey said unsurely, glancing nervously at Jeannie, who glared back ferociously.

"Perfect," Jordyn said with a hard look at Jeannie. She marched to the cold case at the front of the store, grabbed a bottle of Mountain Dew, marched back across the wood floors and shoved it into Kelsey's hands. "There you go. I'll see you tomorrow." Then, more for Jeannie's benefit than his own, Kelsey thought, she gave him a quick hot kiss on the cheek. For the second time in a few short minutes, he was stunned into silence.

Kelsey wandered bemusedly out the front door. He heard Jordyn's angry voice and Jeannie's equally heated one begin to shout over each other as the door swung shut.

...

The next afternoon he hadn't even had time to close his truck door before Jordyn came out of her house. He leaned against the vehicle and watched her approach. He had never seen anything so wildly beautiful. The desert wind blew her dark hair in riotous waves as she skipped lightly down the porch steps in cutoff shorts and a loose black t-shirt. She flashed him a bright smile as she crossed the distance between them in a few breezy strides. He closed his mouth and swallowed hard, hoping she hadn't noticed his gawking stare.

Without saying a word, Jordyn stood on tiptoes and kissed his cheek lightly. Then she moved around the open truck door and slid in, over the driver's seat and into the middle. She settled herself and looked up at him expectantly, a slight smile moving her cheeks. Kelsey, struck dumb by her confidence, nodded slightly as a slow smile stretched across his face.

"Hello to you too, Darlin'," he said, his voice low and smooth.

She laughed shortly and patted the seat next to her. Kelsey jumped in effortlessly and slammed the door.

"Where to?" Jordyn asked lightly.

"Well..." Kelsey trailed off, suddenly feeling very self-conscious, an unfamiliar feeling. "I thought maybe we could go to the Happy Burro for dinner?" Kelsey swallowed hard again, feeling very stupid.

The Happy Burro? Really? Kelsey mentally kicked himself for ever thinking the Happy Burro was a good idea. He chanced a glance at her face and found a smile.

"Kelsey, there is nothing more I would like than to go to the Happy Burro with you." Kelsey noted the amusement in her tone and felt like crawling into a hole. Before he could try to redeem himself, she spoke again. "It's a little early for dinner though. Maybe we could go to the shop you work at?" It was her turn to sound unsure.

Kelsey looked at her fully now, a question in his eyes. "How did you know where I worked?"

"I asked around," she said as she bit her lip. "I know your boss, Steve. He comes in every morning for biscuits and gravy." She almost sounded apologetic. When Kelsey didn't say anything, she continued more nervously. "I don't even know how we got on the subject about you. But he says you are the best help he's ever had. He said you know a ton about cars and that I should come by the shop sometime if I was interested." She looked down at her hands, then back up into his eyes.

"Well," Kelsey said, his usual apathetic attitude warring with the happiness he felt at her caring enough to ask about him. "I hope you didn't ask too many questions." A dark shadow crossed his field of vision as he realized she could easily find out exactly the type of guy he was. The corners of his mouth hardened.

"No, not too many," she replied, briefly frowning at the hard look on his face.

Don't ruin this now, Kelsey, he thought. *Just give it a chance.*

He took a steady breath. "I'll take you by the shop. Sure."

"It's alright if you don't want to. I don't need to go right now. It's just—"

"I love that you cared enough to ask about me," Kelsey found himself saying in another burst of emotion. He expected her to laugh at him this time. She didn't.

Nodding slowly, she said, "I did. And I do. Care, I mean."

He let her words soak into him like a desert rain.

He reached for her hand. Their fingertips touched, sending a bolt of lightning through the middle of his chest. He slowly twined his fingers through hers, feeling every millimeter of skin joining together.

"Well," Kelsey heard his gruff voice say, "then let's go to the shop."

"Let's." Her answering smile was warm and light. She squeezed his hand.

Steve's 1997 Chevy Suburban was gone when they pulled up to the single-level, dusty white building that sat along the main road through Beatty. Steve always left a light on in the shop and one in the office to make it look like someone was around. Kelsey cut the engine and nodded toward the building.

"Here we are. Still want to check it out?" He couldn't keep the excitement out of his voice. This was a part of him he'd never shared with anyone except Steve.

"Of course!" Jordyn bumped his shoulder lightly with her own.

Kelsey offered her a hand to help her from the truck. She took it and didn't break their hold as they walked up to the door to the office. Kelsey's heart skipped as he felt her fingers wind through his. When they reached the door, Kelsey took out a key, unlocked the door and pushed it open. It stuck slightly. A small bell tinkled overhead. He flipped on all of the lights.

"It's not much but..." Kelsey paused. "Well, it's kind of home to me."

Jordyn flashed him a sweet smile and walked toward the computer. She ran her hand absently along the laminate surface of the desk and tilted her head to check out the small room just beyond the filing cabinets.

"Bathroom," said Kelsey. "If you need it."

Jordyn smiled and looked into his eyes again. "I'm fine."

Kelsey's heart flipped over as he felt the heat radiating from her eyes. It was too much to be alone under a roof with this woman. He was beginning to think he wouldn't be able to keep his promise to Steve. He needed a distraction.

"Do you want to see the shop?" Kelsey nodded his head to where a door stood ajar.

"Sure."

She came around the desk, took his hand again and he led her into the shop. The shop had a single bay with enough room to accommodate cupboards along either side. A faded purple Pontiac Grand Am was jacked six feet up on the car lift in the center. A bright industrial light on the work bench next to them cast strange shadows across the shop floor. When Jordyn released his hand to investigate the odds and ends on the bench, Kelsey walked up to the Pontiac. He put his hand on the tire that hovered next to his forehead.

"You didn't hear this from me, but these cars are garbage." His voice reverberated around the cement-floored shop.

"Oh yea?" Jordyn said in a playfully defensive tone. "I kind of always wanted one."

Kelsey gave her a disgusted look that made her laugh.

"Seriously!" she said. "I think they look pretty cool."

Kelsey let out a breath through his lips. "This is your dream car?"

"Well, no," she replied slowly. "I mean, maybe... I just haven't put much thought into it, I guess." She looked up at him to gage his reaction. When she met Kelsey's incredulous stare, she said hotly, "Okay, Mr. Mechanic, what's your dream car?"

"'81 Red Ford Mustang Cobra, 4.2 liter, V8," Kelsey replied without hesitation.

Jordyn had her mouth open to say something biting in return but his quick reply left her speechless. Something about the way she stared at him made him feel self-conscious.

"My mom had that car. I've always wanted one." Kelsey shrugged.

The look on Jordyn's face transformed into something unreadable. He distracted himself by examining a hang nail on his finger.

"You should get one then," Jordyn said at last, her voice soft.

Kelsey looked up from his hand into her face and a smile spread across his own.

"I've been looking," he said more enthusiastically than he would've liked.

She smiled in return. "Oh yea?"

"Yea. I check Autotrader at least once a week. I've almost saved enough."

"That's amazing," Jordyn replied genuinely.

"I know. It's taken me two and a half years."

They both smiled at each other. Neither spoke for a few moments.

Kelsey broke the silence, "Well, should we—"

"Yes. Let's go to the Happy Burro," Jordyn finished for him.

As they entered the office from the shop, Jordyn grasped his arm. "Have you checked Autotrader this week?" she asked.

"No, I haven't," Kelsey replied. "But it's okay. I'll look tomorrow."

"Let's check now. I want to see what one looks like."

Kelsey couldn't help the huge grin that spread over his face. "Okay," he said and squeezed her hand.

He led her around to the computer. He sat down in the spinning chair and she leaned lightly on the back of his shoulders. Her warm breath ruffled the hair on his head. The sensation made Kelsey briefly forget how to open the computer. He took a deep breath to clear his head and clicked the glowing letter 'e'.

Autotrader popped up and he tapped absently on the keys. The search engine was taking too long. Kelsey began to feel impatient and acutely aware of Jordyn's body close behind his shoulders. Her breath began to warm the top of his head. He closed his eyes and inhaled deeply, trying to keep his mind on the task at hand.

"What about that red one?" Jordyn said suddenly. His eyes snapped open and saw her finger hovering over a new listing.

"1981 Red Ford Mustang Cobra, $10,995."

Slowly, his finger pressed down on the mouse. A small click brought the new page up.

Kelsey blinked once and started to read.

"Look," Jordyn interrupted his reading. "It's in Indian Springs. That's only an hour away." She paused. "And it's at Silver Springs Industries Auto Shop. They fixed it up really nice... well, except for a small oil leak." She gripped his shoulder. "We should go see it!"

Kelsey didn't say anything while he finished reading what Jordyn had relayed to him. He could not believe he had found one close to home. And it was below what he had expected to pay. His heart jumped into his chest and he felt his legs flex to move. Before he could jump up, something occurred to him and he stopped.

"Damn it," he said angrily to himself, momentarily forgetting Jordyn was there. He whipped his head around self-consciously. She stood behind him unperturbed.

"Damn it, what?" she asked.

"Oh, well, I still don't have the money saved for it."

She stared at him as if he were speaking another language.

He frowned. "What?"

"I don't see a problem," she replied simply.

"It's pointless to go see it. I can't buy it."

"Come on, Kels. Live a little. I bet they are still open. If not, it'll be a nice drive."

It was Kelsey's turn to stare at her. She blinked twice and raised her eyebrows.

"Did you just call me Kels?" he asked.

"Yea, I guess," she said. "Why?"

"Only my sister calls me that."

She looked down at her shoes. "I'm sorry, I—"

"No." Kelsey stood up quickly and grabbed her hand. "I like it. That's a good thing. It just...threw me, is all."

She looked up at him through her lashes and studied his face. "Alright then...Kels." She tested the nickname slowly. She seemed happy with his reaction because she smiled. "So, can we go?" she said brightly.

Kelsey shook his head and unsuccessfully suppressed a smile as he watched her bounce lightly on the balls of her feet. "How can I say no?"

With a dazzling smile, she led him out the door.

Three miles down the highway her feet were stretched out on the passenger side of the bench seat. Her back was pressed to his arm. The fanned air blasted through the cab of the truck, doing little to cool their sticky bodies. He could feel sweat pooling where the skin of his arm touched the t-shirt on her back. Kelsey cared little about the heat and sweat. He was focused only on the woman next to him.

His whole world shifted when he was around her. In her presence, his horrible excuse for a life seemed worth living. He glanced over the top of Jordyn's head and wondered if she felt the same way. Kelsey mentally kicked himself. It was only their first date; of course she didn't feel the same way. As if reading his thoughts, she turned her face up to him, displaying a peaceful smile. She reached for the stereo knobs.

"Do you mind?" she asked.

"Go ahead."

Garth Brooks's smooth country twang filled the cab as she turned it up. Brooks's song, 'The Dance' was instantly recognizable. Kelsey wasn't usually a fan of ballads, but with Jordyn's weight pressed against his shoulder, he sat contentedly appreciating the song for the first time. The desert blurred past their windows as Jordyn let her head rest against his shoulder.

Chapter 6

KELSEY SHIFTED HIMSELF and draped his arm over the back of the bench seat. Jordyn drew her knees up and his fingers lightly grazed the tops. After a few minutes of stillness, Kelsey wondered if she'd fallen asleep. He stretched his neck to sneak a look down at her face. She stirred and peaked up at him.

"You alright?" Kelsey asked.

"I sure am," she said serenely. "I can't tell you when I've ever felt this relaxed."

Kelsey smiled. "Me too."

She returned the smile, then reached her face up to kiss him on his cheek. Her lips left an icy hot sensation. Kelsey's smile widened.

"What was that for?" he asked.

"I'm just happy," she replied and settled back into her spot on his arm.

Kelsey continued to grin even though she couldn't see his face and wondered if he could bottle happiness like this.

The small town of Indian Springs loomed on the horizon much earlier than Kelsey would have liked. He wondered if she would notice if he kept on driving south toward Las Vegas and beyond. He wondered if she would keep her back pressed into him, head lolling on his shoulder while they rode on through the night. He wondered if she would balk at him if he suggested it.

He felt her move and she swung her legs around onto the floor boards. She flipped the radio off and leaned forward in her seat, stretching.

"That went fast," she said, echoing his own thoughts. "I've never really been here, have you?"

"No," Kelsey replied. "But by the look of it, there isn't much to see."

She nodded as the truck slowed into town.

"There it is," she said, pointing to a building that looked almost identical to Steve's Auto Shop.

Instead of 'Steve's' printed in scrawling cursive red letters, 'Silver Springs Industries' was printed in chunky black letters over the entrance to the big garage doors. Kelsey turned the truck onto the pavement in front of the shop. No lights were on inside and all the doors appeared to be sealed for the evening.

"We must've missed them," Jordyn said. "Let's go look through the window to see if the Mustang is in there."

Kelsey opened the door and helped Jordyn down. She stretched her arms overhead and adjusted the t-shirt over her chest. He felt the corner of his mouth turn up. She caught his smirk and poked him in the arm playfully.

"C'mon." She grabbed his hand and pulled him to the windowed rolling door of the shop.

Kelsey shaded his eyes against the evening sun and looked in. An older Jeep Cherokee sat in the center of the dark shop. Straining his eyes further, he found no Mustang. He felt his heart sink. He hadn't realized he was counting on it being there.

"I don't—" Kelsey began but was interrupted by a whoosh and a muffled thud. He looked toward the business office side of the building just as a man emerged.

The man looked first at Kelsey's truck, then over at Kelsey and Jordyn. He nodded his head and quickly walked toward them. Kelsey returned the nod.

"How can I help you kids?" the man asked, his groomed mechanics beard curled around a toothy smile.

Kelsey instantly bristled at being referred to as a kid. This man didn't look that much older than Kelsey himself. From what he could tell under the oil grease that covered most of the man's exposed skin, he was maybe thirty. The man was shorter than Kelsey and scrawnier. After the quick size up, Kelsey decided he could easily take this guy out. He crossed his arms steadily over his chest.

In a classic double take that set Kelsey's teeth on edge, the man acknowledged Jordyn. He held her gaze longer than Kelsey liked.

"We saw an ad for a Mustang," Kelsey said firmly, his voice demanding the man's attention. The man's grey-blue eyes parted reluctantly from Jordyn's face.

"Yes!" the man said enthusiastically. "Sold it this morning. I meant to take it off Autotrader but didn't have the time." Kelsey felt his lungs deflate as the man continued, "Nice guy from Las Vegas bought it for his 16-year-old daughter. He paid cash and—" Glancing back at Jordyn, the man interrupted himself. "I'm sorry, but have we met before?"

Kelsey hadn't looked at Jordyn since the man came out of the office but glanced at her now. Although the man was obviously addressing her, she was looking away as if she hadn't heard him. Her hair ruffled around her face, hiding it from his view.

"The name's Wade. You just look so familiar," the man named Wade insisted, slightly craning his neck forward to look closer at her.

Although Kelsey didn't know this man, Kelsey recognized a smile that he had seen on many men's faces when they looked at a woman. It was one he wore himself occasionally. His stomach hardened. His fingers twitched.

As Wade continued to stare, she turned her face toward him, unable to ignore his probing gaze. Her face was unreadable. She neither smiled or frowned but examined him coolly. He continued to smile at her, still too interested.

"No," she said quietly but firmly, even her voice unreadable. "I don't believe we've met."

"Alright. If you're sure. I just—" Wade interrupted himself for the second time. His eyes widened. His mouth popped open a few centimeters and silently shut again, reminding Kelsey of a goldfish he had watched die on the bathroom floor as a kid. Jordyn shifted uneasily under his gaze and Kelsey felt his irritation peak.

As suddenly as his face changed, Wade regained his composure. An odd grin peaked from under his beard. "As I was saying," he said slowly, still watching Jordyn. "The Mustang is gone." He glanced at Kelsey. "Sorry," he added lamely.

"That's fine," Kelsey said quickly. "Let's go." Kelsey spun on his heels and started toward the truck. He felt Jordyn follow him.

He'd taken two steps when he heard Jordyn's quick intake of breath. Kelsey whirled and saw that Wade had stepped in front of Jordyn. His eyes were glinting with fire and locked on her face only inches from his own.

"I do know you," he hissed at her through his teeth. He was smiling though his tone was dark.

Kelsey crossed the distance between them in a half stride. He grabbed Wade's wrist and twisted it behind his back. Wade gave a loud yelp of pain. Kelsey brought his knee up hard into Wade's groin. Wade doubled over, his mouth opening and closing like the dying fish. Kelsey shoved violently on the twisted arm and sent Wade sprawling backward onto the pavement. Kelsey thought he heard a bone crack and wasn't disappointed when Wade sat up holding his arm and wincing in pain.

"What the hell, man?" Wade said, squinting up at him. "You know what girls like that are like."

"You shut your god-damn mouth before I kick it shut," Kelsey threatened, his voice sounding like a growl in his ears. He could feel his chest vibrating in anger. His fingers flexed, and his thighs tensed. He took a step forward. Wade didn't open his mouth to speak or move to get up. Kelsey glared at him, chest heaving with rage and adrenaline. The muscles in his leg ached to swing forward and cave Wade's bearded face in.

A soft touch on his shoulder made his heart skip. He impulsively shrugged off Jordyn's hand. She sucked in a quick breath. Kelsey glanced back, thinking he had hurt her. Her pleading eyes met his for a moment. Anger at Wade was warring violently with the vision of the imploring green eyes behind him. He took a deep breath and exhaled slowly. With a hard look at Wade, Kelsey used every amount of self-control he possessed and turned away from him.

"Let's go," he said through clenched jaw, avoiding her eyes.

His anger felt as though it was visibly boiling off his skin. His whole body felt like a coiled spring. Every muscle rippled with unreleased tension. Only when Jordyn slid in beside him and the door was shut did he feel his chest muscles loosen. Still without looking at Jordyn, he crammed the keys into the ignition and brought the truck to life. He stepped hard on the gas. The tires flicked bits of rock behind them as they pulled recklessly onto the highway.

Ten long minutes passed without sound or movement from either of them. Jordyn sat on the far side of the bench seat now, feet firmly on the floor and knees pressed together. Her face was turned down and unreadable. Kelsey gripped the steering wheel with both hands, right foot still pressed deeply on the gas pedal. His free foot tapped mindlessly on the floor panel. His eyes flicked back and forth on the road, replaying the last moments with Wade.

A slow-moving semi-truck in front of them caused Kelsey to slow down. The change in his frenetic speed slowed his heart. As his heart decelerated, so did his anger. Finally, his head cleared like a departing sandstorm. He became acutely aware of the tense woman beside him.

He spoke with what he hoped was a light tone. "What the hell was that about?" He chanced a glance at Jordyn.

She ducked her head and twisted her fingers together. "I... I—" she began in a whisper.

"I mean, what a dick!" Kelsey interrupted. "I should've broken his nose and his arm." One of his fists slammed against the steering wheel in a stirring of the rage that floated close to the surface.

Jordyn didn't respond. Kelsey looked at her. Her shoulders were hunched. Huge silent tears fell from her eyes onto her lap. A wave of sick regret filled Kelsey's stomach and sat like a lead weight there.

"Oh, Darlin'. I'm so sorry." Kelsey pulled the truck into a convenient turnout on the highway. A sedan behind them honked furiously at the quick exit. Ignoring the sedan, he pushed the gear into Neutral and reached across the seat, not quite touching her. "I'm so sorry." More tears splashed onto the fabric of her cutoff jean shorts. "I was so angry. I'm so sorry."

Jordyn reached a finger up to brush her tears away. They were instantly replaced by new ones. She didn't respond or reach for his outstretched hand.

Kelsey pressed back into his seat, letting his head fall against the window. He knew he'd done the one thing that he had tried not to do — he had shown his true colors. The worst part was that his anger was only the beginning of his issues. She had only just begun to see the worst in him. Rightfully so, she was crying and most likely scared of him.

Questions swirled in his head and blurred his vision. Why hadn't he tried to talk to the guy? Why had he broken the guy's arm? Why was he unable to control himself? Why was he so much like his dad?

A cool hand touched his. Kelsey looked down at it, then up her arm and into her eyes. The tears were wiped away, but more were waiting to spill down her cheeks. She pressed her lips together, obviously trying to hold her emotion in, but she still held her gaze steadily on his.

"I'm sorry too," she said quietly, her lips barely moving.

Kelsey had not been expecting this. He sucked in a quick breath and let it out, at a loss for words.

"I'm sorry, Kelsey," she continued. A tear jumped onto her cheek.

Watching the tear roll down her face filled him with new anger. But anger at himself this time. He found his words.

"No," he said, matching her volume but magnifying her intensity. "You will not be sorry for how I acted. This has nothing to do with you." He watched her face to see that she was receptive. Pleased that she appeared to be, he continued, "I told you I was not a good guy in high school. Well, that never changed. And in a lot of ways, I'm worse. Much worse. You just got to witness that. I'm just not..." He trailed off, unable to say the words that he should have said.

I'm just not good for you.

Those words cut to his core. He couldn't break this off now, even if it was the right thing to do. His eyes fell to the seat where their hands sat unmoving. The cab of the truck was silent for a full minute.

"Have you ever raped a woman?" Jordyn's soft words caused Kelsey to jerk his head up. He frowned at her. She raised an eyebrow, apparently waiting for a serious answer.

"No," he replied definitively.

Just slept with every hooker in town, he thought miserably.

"Have you ever killed anyone?" Jordyn asked seriously.

"No."

But I want to murder my dad nearly every day.

"Do you do any hard drugs?" she asked.

"No."

Just drink myself to sleep nearly every night.

Jordyn pressed her lips together. "Well, then. With those basic questions out of the way, I think my safety is not seriously in question at this point. And, if you don't mind, I'd like to figure out all the other ways you think you're not a good guy for myself." She raised her eyebrow again, stunning him into silence.

After a minute, Kelsey let out a long breath and shook his head. "I don't know what to say."

"Then don't," she replied and squeezed his hand.

"What now?" Kelsey asked, at a loss for the next step.

She paused before answering. "Well, the Happy Burro will be closed by the time we get back to Beatty." Her bright green eyes flashed to his own and the hint of a smile stirred her lips. He felt a tiny bubble of laughter pop in his chest. It spread light throughout his body.

"So..." she continued, "we should probably just head back home. I think I saw a market in the middle of nowhere out here. We could get something to eat there?"

"Yea. Sounds good."

Two bags of potato chips, a beef jerky chew, two Cokes and a chocolate bar later, Kelsey and Jordyn found themselves contentedly enjoying the passing sage brush. Few cars were on the highway this evening. For the first time he could remember, Kelsey let his foot barely rest on the gas pedal. The Ford purred at a slower pace, right at the speed limit, and Kelsey felt renewed by the soothing sound of the engine.

Jordyn rested her head on his shoulder. He loved the feel of her silken hair against his skin. He let his cheek rest against the top of her head. She pressed her own cheek firmly into his shoulder. He could see the skin around her eyes creasing in a smile.

The sun fell below the horizon. This minute after sunset was Kelsey's favorite time. In those few moments when the earth still remembered the life-giving light of the sun, the world surged with a final rush of energy. The horizon glowed bright white. The sky shone with brilliant bursts of yellow and orange. The rocks, trees and brush fell reverently silent and still. The whole land sent a final farewell to the sun as if saying thank you for the day.

The cab of the truck quickly fell into darkness as the sun sank lower and the desert around them turned the inky black of a moonless night. It was peaceful and quiet apart from the low rumble of the engine.

"Are your momma and sister going to miss you?" Kelsey asked, almost hating the sound of his voice breaking into the serene space around them.

"No." Her voice came soft from his shoulder. "They are used to me being gone."

Something in her tone made him wonder if she had been crying again.

"Do you work a lot at night then?" Kelsey asked lightly, hoping to avoid whatever was making her emotional. "I mean, you said you mostly worked morning shifts. They must have a lot of shifts to pick up at the market?"

"Yea," she replied simply and quietly.

Kelsey still sensed that something was wrong, but didn't want to push it further. Luckily, he was good at being silent and chose that course of action. He didn't deserve any kind of inter-action with her anyway. He had blown that today. His wildest hope at this point was that she would wake up the next morning and still want to see him.

The time passed slowly and before he was ready, Kelsey turned onto the long drive that led to her house. Her neighbors all appeared to be awake, their televisions casting unnatural blue light from their windows into the darkness outside. In contrast, Jordyn's house was dark except for a dim orb of light shining through a drawn curtain on the far end of the mobile home. Jordyn sat straighter when she saw it.

"My Lizzie," she said. "She likes to look at picture books in the evening." Kelsey could hear a sweet smile in her voice. "I've found her up until midnight looking at pictures of butterflies."

"She seems real sweet," Kelsey replied as he put the truck in Neutral and looked across at her darkened face.

"She is." Jordyn looked at him, her green eyes sparkling in the light of the truck's glowing green radio buttons.

Kelsey reached across and grasped both of her hands lightly. "Look. This wasn't a great first date." Kelsey swallowed hard and she smirked. "I definitely don't deserve to see you again and part of me thinks I shouldn't...but—"

Jordyn reached her face up to press her lips lightly to his own. The kiss was brief but effectively silenced him. He forgot what he was about to say and where he was. His body relaxed for the first time since he'd knocked Wade down. He brought a hand lightly up to touch her cheek and ran his thumb down the skin of her jaw. It was warm and smooth.

"Jordyn, I—" Kelsey began, but was loudly interrupted by his cell phone ringing obnoxiously from his front pocket. Tinny electronic beeps and twangs bounced around the truck and he frantically grabbed at his pants to pull it out, cursing under his breath. Jordyn giggled.

"God, it's my sister," Kelsey said when he finally fished it from his jeans and squinted at the tiny caller ID. His thumb automatically curled over the green answer key.

"Go ahead," Jordyn said, still giggling. "Get it. I need to go see if Lizzie is okay anyway."

"But—" Kelsey started to protest as the phone continued its piercing ring.

"It's okay. I'll see you around." Jordyn replied and kissed his cheek, leaving a warm imprint.

She opened the truck door and swung her legs out. Giving him a quick wave and shy smile, she slammed the door and jogged toward her house. Kelsey watched as he reluctantly pressed the answer button.

"Hey," he said familiarly into the cell phone, watching Jordyn disappear into the house and feeling that new sensation of his heart leaving with her. His sister's sing-song voice filled his ear and it took a moment for him to respond. "What do you mean I sound weird?"

Chapter 7

"I MEAN YOU SOUND DIFFERENT. Sort of odd," Kelsey's sister, Anne, spoke playfully over the phone. "If I didn't know better I would say you maybe sounded... happy?"

In faux exasperation, Kelsey let out an audible breath and shoved the '92 into gear while pinning the cell phone between his ear and shoulder. With one last glance at Jordyn's house he pulled down the lane toward the highway.

"Well, if you must know," he said, exaggerating his annoyance, "I was with a woman."

"Oh, Jesus Christ, Kels, please tell me you aren't actually with a woman right now."

"For god's sake, I wouldn't answer the phone if I were." Kelsey rolled his eyes even though she was on the phone and hundreds of miles away. "What you must think of me."

"I think a lot about you," she replied. "And don't roll your eyes at me."

Kelsey laughed shortly.

"Anyway, you must like this woman by the sound of it," Anne said, her tone implying that she wanted to continue the conversation.

"Let's just leave it for now. Eh, Sis?" Kelsey sped onto the highway.

"Brad called," Anne said, the playfulness suddenly gone from her voice.

"What for this time?" Kelsey felt heat creep up his neck at the mention of his dad's name.

"Asking about my mom again."

"What the hell?"

"I know. He won't get over her." Anne paused. "Though I couldn't tell you why," she continued darkly.

"Is she bad again?" Kelsey asked, feeling the happiness he'd felt with Jordyn draining away with each passing second.

"When is she not bad?" Anne replied. "I haven't seen her in two weeks."

"God, Anne. Why didn't you call sooner? Do you need anything?"

"No, I'm actually doing good. I got a different job. And I'm crashing at my friend's apartment for a while. I haven't even been to my mom's place since she tweaked out the last time." Anne sounded brighter. Kelsey felt a heaviness settle in his stomach.

"Who is this friend? And why don't you get the hell out of that city?" Kelsey gripped the steering wheel.

"Sacramento is fine if you know where to avoid," Anne said soothingly. "And the friend is just that. A friend. She works with me at the café where I got a job."

Kelsey grunted in reply.

"Really, Kels. It's fine. I just miss you. I'm going to visit soon."

"I should come there," Kelsey said resolutely.

"No. You would get so lost here," she teased. "I need to meet this woman of yours anyway."

"Annie, I said drop it." Kelsey tried to sound serious, but failed. His sister had his heart strings.

"No one calls me Annie here," she said with a note of regret in her voice. "I do miss you."

"Come anytime, Sis."

"I will," she said. "Soon."

"Love you," Kelsey said softly.

"Love you too, Kels." The line clicked off.

Kelsey drew in a deep breath and watched the lights of the town of Beatty pass by in a slow blur. His sister was the only brightness in his dark life. Although she was two years younger than him, they'd been inseparable since she could walk. Anne had been born only a month after Kelsey's own mom died from a drug overdose. Though Kelsey couldn't remember for himself, Anne's mom, Delilah, once told him that he had stayed by Anne's side every waking moment from the time she was born.

Delilah moved in with Brad less than a week after Kelsey's mom, Laura, died. Delilah was hugely pregnant with Anne at the time and took Laura's place in their home as if nothing had happened. From the time Kelsey could remember, Delilah was on some sort of illicit drug. When she wasn't stripping to earn money for drugs, she was in her room, too far gone to interact with her daughter or Kelsey. She would watch the children with the mildly amused interest of one watching a cheap television program. After Anne was old enough to dress herself, Kelsey never remembered Delilah preparing meals for them, taking them anywhere or helping with school. The kids were left on their own. Brad didn't care what Delilah was doing as long as she stayed out of his way and didn't stop him from visiting the brothel or drinking through all their money.

Kelsey could remember two times that Delilah had attempted to give up drugs. The first attempt uneventfully ended less than twenty-four hours after it began. The second resulted in her moving out of the house, dragging a crying sixteen-year-old Anne with her. Kelsey had not seen Delilah since, though Anne came to visit twice a year for the past three years.

Initially, Brad barely noticed that Delilah had left. But after a week of her absence, Brad began to obsess about the woman he had ignored for 16 years. He became increasingly irritable, even after drinking. This bad temper only worsened after the accident at the shop a month after Delilah left.

Brad had been working under a two-wheel drive Nissan truck when the jack holding it up failed. The falling truck missed killing him outright, but he'd ended up with a broken back that permanently crippled him. In his time spent healing, Brad became totally unreachable. In Brad's mind, Delilah was both the one who got away and the reason for his broken body. And, after the accident, Kelsey avoided him at all cost.

Kelsey spoke with Anne on the phone at least once a week since she'd moved with Delilah to Sacramento. They cared deeply for each other and shared everything. Delilah relapsed within days of moving to Sacramento and Kelsey had been Anne's only lifeline. Anne had not finished high school after being ripped from Beatty High School before her junior year, so she was forced to work part-time at fast food joints in order to get the money for clothes and food for herself. Delilah still worked as a stripper to pay for her drug habit and sometimes the rent.

During one of their many phone calls, Anne warned Kelsey about their dad. Delilah had confessed to Anne during one of her lucid moments that Brad had regularly threatened to harm the kids if she didn't stay out of his way. In a drunk state one night, Brad had told Delilah that he would kill Anne and Kelsey if she didn't kill herself first. He'd told her that he was done with her and ready to move on. This had been the impetus for her departure.

Kelsey listened to Anne's warning about Brad, but took everything Delilah said with a healthy dose of skepticism. Even if what Delilah said was true, Kelsey figured he was grown and strong enough, and Brad old enough and injured enough that he wasn't a threat. Kelsey still avoided Brad, but mostly because he was impossible to live with and because Brad reminded him of how alike they were.

The dim blue glow of the television peeked through the curtains of the mobile home as he pulled down the long driveway. Kelsey hoped Brad was asleep. He wasn't disappointed. Brad was in his recliner, mouth open, eyes closed, breathing heavily. The television murmured indistinctly from the corner.

Kelsey passed into the kitchen. He flipped the light on above the stove. It cast a yellow glow around the cluttered space. Kelsey grabbed a beer from the refrigerator and popped it open on the counter in a practiced movement. Walking to his bedroom, his foot kicked an empty beer bottle. It careened noisily across the kitchen floor and into the cupboard on the opposite side. A jolting memory of another beer bottle spinning across the floor made him pause.

In his memory, Kelsey was four years old and Anne only two. They were playing with an empty beer bottle on the linoleum floor of this same kitchen. He remembered spinning it in circles and laughing with her as the bottle slid across the floor, bumping into the wooden chair legs and walls. They continued playing until the chair in front of them was lifted up and smashed against the wall just one foot to their left. Dislodged wooden legs flung around the room.

He remembered looking up in surprise to see Brad. His dad's face was crimson red with drink and his eyes shone black from behind his sun-browned skin. Anne's little face had looked at Brad too. She'd blinked once then turned and crawled toward her bedroom, chubby legs slipping on the floor as she scrambled away in fear. Kelsey remained frozen in place, however, knowing he should follow his sister but unable to move. He remembered Brad's mouth curving into a grimacing smile before the room went black. The memory of that day ended as quickly as it had come, but Kelsey ran his hand along the scar above his right eye, etched there by Brad's boot seventeen years ago.

Kelsey glanced impulsively into the living room where Brad slept, undisturbed by the beer bottle Kelsey had kicked. Tonight, there was no whiskey bottle next to him — just beer.

Thank god, Kelsey thought.

It had been whiskey that day in the kitchen with Anne and the beer bottle. Brad was relatively docile when he drank beer, which was from dawn to far into the night. Being drunk was his natural state. When he drank beer at least he kept to himself, but not so with whiskey. He only drank whiskey when he was thinking about Kelsey's mom, Laura. And when he drank it, he drank it fast. It was minutes before he became unreachable, untouchable and uncontrollable. His anger and volume built like an erupting volcano, spewing insults, accusations and violent blows in a 360-degree circle around him. That day seventeen years ago was his first memory of Brad's volatility when he drank whiskey — but it wasn't his only one.

Kelsey stalked off to his bedroom. He felt the change in his mood like a thunder storm. It had been less than a half hour since he'd dropped Jordyn off and he'd felt so happy. He hadn't thought anything could take that feeling away; yet here he was, sucked back into the endless vortex of his bleak life.

The only way he knew how to deal with the uncertainty and anger was clutched tightly in his hand. The cool damp exterior of the bottle felt like a security blanket. He drank deeply as he lay on his bed. Finally, after completing his eighth trip to the refrigerator, Kelsey let the numbing waves of drink carry him to sleep.

Chapter 8

KELSEY WOKE THE NEXT morning, squinting at the brightness streaming in through the open window. His first thought was one of excitement. Happy memories of the day before made his heart skip and a small smile stretch his features. Just as quickly, he remembered the other memories of the day before. The man called Wade, his anger and the unsureness he felt about Jordyn made him close his eyes, wishing he hadn't woken at all. Eventually, the only thing that propelled him out of bed was the knowledge that Steve would be waiting for him at the shop with a day's worth of work in which to bury himself.

As he pulled into his parking spot at Steve's shop, Kelsey noticed a small red Nissan Sentra parked outside with someone sitting in it. Steve didn't usually leave customers waiting. Kelsey approached the Nissan. His heart jumped and caught in his throat as the door opened.

"Hi, Kels," Jordyn said shyly as the Nissan's door shut softly behind her.

Kelsey opened his mouth but his voice caught for a moment. "Hi."

Jordyn pushed her hair back behind her ear and ducked her head, speaking to her hands. "I thought you might worry about me not wanting to see you again after yesterday." She looked up from her hands, her eyes searching his face. "I just want you to know that I'd like to see you again."

Kelsey nodded stupidly, unsure of how to respond. How had she read his mind? A slow smile spread across his face.

"Anyway, I've got to get to work. I just wanted you to know that." Jordyn ducked her head again and reached for the faded black handle of the Nissan's car door.

"Wait." Kelsey reached involuntarily for her, stopping her arm. "Thank you."

Her answering smile lit the morning on fire. He returned it.

She climbed in and shut the door. Kelsey's hand fell to the top of the car and rested there while she started it up. Glancing at him, she rolled the window down.

"See you later?" she asked.

"Yes," Kelsey answered eagerly. "I get off at 5:30."

"Perfect. My house?"

"I'll be there."

Kelsey felt a swell of amusement in his chest. He smirked.

"What?" she asked warily.

"I didn't know you cared so much about me," Kelsey said.

A flash of something serious crossed her eyes before she squinted them coyly. "There's a lot you don't know about me, Kelsey Campbell." She pushed the Nissan into gear and the car disappeared from under Kelsey's hand.

...

Over the next two weeks, they saw each other every day. She asked about his family, his work, his interests and his dreams. Kelsey felt himself consumed entirely by her. Each moment he wasn't engrossed in work he was thinking about her. She made him feel that life was worth it; and, if he dared think it, she made him feel loved.

He was completely open with her about his family past. He talked freely about Brad, Anne and his mom. He discussed his anger with his dad. In a particularly vulnerable moment, he revealed to her that he sometimes wondered if Brad had murdered his mom. Even as he spoke the words, he knew it was crazy, that it had been a drug overdose. Her death hadn't been a surprise to anyone, since his momma was a known prostitute and drug addict. Jordyn had listened and cried silently as he talked.

Kelsey felt safe enough around her to reveal that he had a terrible relationship with beer, just like Brad. Somehow, talking about it made it easier to control himself after he left her. Consumed as he was with her presence, he simply forgot to drink in the evenings.

There was one thing he hadn't talked to Jordyn about — one thing he couldn't, one thing that she wouldn't forgive him for. He couldn't bring himself to tell her about his visits to the brothel. Although he hadn't visited the Desert Rose Angels since their first date, the fresh knowledge that he regularly partook of the Angels' services felt like a betrayal in some way. He wanted to tell her. He wanted to share every part of himself, but the fear of losing her forever kept him silent.

Kelsey was also able to ask about her family and past. She talked lightly with him about her sister's Down syndrome and her mama's drug addiction. Kelsey listened attentively while Jordyn talked about the challenges and many joys of living with a sister with Down syndrome. They understood without words what it was like to live with an addict parent. Jordyn didn't talk about her dad because neither she nor her mother knew who he was.

He learned that she loved to read. She read every book she could get her hands on, from science textbooks to romance novels. Between working every shift the market offered and homeschooling her sister, she had little time for anything else. She claimed that reading was her drug of choice, an escape from daily life.

Jordyn explained that she had to work a lot to support her family. The state of Nevada paid Supplemental Security Income for Lizzie and some welfare for her mom; but, according to Jordyn, it wasn't enough to pay the bills or give Lizzie the life she deserved — especially since a lot of that money ended up in her mom's dealer's pocket. Since Jordyn was the only able person in their house, it was her job to keep everyone fed and under a solid roof. Her attitude about this was matter-of-fact. This was the life she knew.

Between Jordyn's shifts at the market and Kelsey's job, and because Brad was ever-present at Kelsey's home and Lizzie at Jordyn's, carpooling to and from their work places was about the only time they could be alone together to talk.

They took turns taking Kelsey's truck and Jordyn's Nissan, but Kelsey felt bittersweet about their arrangement. He was both pleased and wholly frustrated that they had no time to explore the physical side of their relationship. He knew enough about sex to know that he was in grave danger with her. His heart wanted to give her space and respect and something entirely unlike what he'd given the whores he had been with; but his body wanted something different. An uncomfortable fluttering nausea twisted his insides as he wrestled with this clash of logic and desire.

Since she'd kissed him that first night, the only physical contact they'd had was holding hands across the seat and chaste kisses goodbye. Kelsey didn't trust himself at all with her.

Everything about her was perfect and attractive, from her body to her thoughts on life. She was dynamite.

He felt that she was holding back as well. There were moments when the fire in her eyes matched his own, moments when their farewell kisses lingered and the heat blazed between their lips and fingers. In those moments, he felt the catch in her breath, felt the hesitation. Was she protecting herself? Was she still unsure about him?

Regardless of her unspoken feelings toward him, Kelsey took solace in the time they spent together. He knew that, like the inevitable setting of the desert sun, they would have to explore their corporeal desire for each other at some point. But for now, he was content to have her sitting across the truck bench from him, holding his hand in her own.

Three Fridays after their first date, Kelsey sat leaning against the door in the passenger seat of the Nissan Sentra as Jordyn drove him home from a long hot day at the shop. The air conditioner blasted noisily. The vents pointed at his arm and tickled his hair, sending goosebumps up to his shoulders. He smiled as Jordyn sang loudly along with the radio, on at full volume. He waited for the song to end before interrupting her joyous karaoke session.

"Are Friday nights busy at the market?" he asked. Jordyn flicked the radio volume down and glanced quickly at his face, her carefree mood changing to a more serious one.

"Busy enough, I guess," she replied.

"I should steal you away one of these nights. Give you a break," Kelsey said, trying to ease her suddenly darkened features.

"I wish you could," she said earnestly. "But I can't take the time off. Lizzie has another doctor's appointment in Pahrump and I need the money. They need to do some testing on her heart."

"Is everything okay?"

"Oh yea, I think so. Just routine stuff, I guess. I just need the money to pay for the trip there. I usually like to go get her something special after the appointments too. Just a new shirt or book or something. She looks forward to it." Jordyn's cheeks rose in a small smile.

Kelsey smiled faintly back. "You know, if you need some extra money sometime, I can—"

"No," Jordyn interrupted abruptly, her tone firm. She flushed at her intensity. She took a small breath, continuing in a softer voice. "No. I can handle it." She threw him an apologetic smile. "Thank you for the offer though. But you have enough to worry about when it comes to money."

Secretly, Kelsey felt like Jordyn's happiness was far more important than any of the things he had been saving up for, but kept his mouth shut. He couldn't help but notice the firm line that settled around her lips. He wanted to kiss it away. Settling on holding her hand in silence, he shifted himself upright in his seat.

"Hey, do you have anything to drink in here?"

"Yea. Grab my backpack. I have a water bottle in there somewhere."

Kelsey unbuckled and turned halfway around in his seat to grab her backpack. It was surprisingly heavy and it took some considerable force to pull it between the front seats onto his lap. He balanced it on his knees and unzipped the main compartment. The smell of mothballs wafted out of the bag.

"We've got to get you a new backpack," Kelsey said as he dug into the tangle of clothes and unidentified solid objects.

"Hey! I like it." Jordyn swatted playfully at his arm, the hard line around her mouth disappearing. Kelsey smiled, happy to see her mood lighten.

He finally located the water bottle in the dark depths and pulled it roughly out of the bag, causing a book to flop out onto his lap. The cover caught his attention because it was blank. He wondered if it were her diary. He glanced at her to see if she had noticed it fall out.

The cover was thick dark leather, the corners and binding rubbed smooth and shiny, the front and back were coated in fading scratches. There might have been something written on the front at one point, but the leather was too worn to tell. He surreptitiously glanced at the inside page.

A Bible.

He looked at Jordyn in surprise. She caught his look.

"What?" Jordyn looked confused. "Did you find it?"

Kelsey quickly looked away. "Uh yea, I did." He stuffed the Bible back in the bag and zipped it up. He unscrewed the plastic top on the cool metal canteen, tilted it up and drank a few mouthfuls. He screwed the cap back on and swished his last mouthful of water through his teeth, eyeing the backpack.

Jordyn hadn't struck him as a church girl. Sure, she was as good a person as he had ever met, but she had never talked to him about God or going to church. There was no sign of religion at her house or in her room. She didn't behave the way he'd seen church people act — she swore and drank and smoked, and she wore clothes that hugged her in all the right places and showed all the right things. Still, there it was: a small leather book lying hidden in her dirty old backpack, obviously important enough to carry with her everywhere she went.

Kelsey suppressed a derisive grunt. He certainly wasn't a church guy. Brad had dragged Anne and Kelsey to church for a handful of Sundays when he was in sixth grade. Brad had been evangelized by a television preacher during a sober moment and decided that they all needed to be going to church. This brief stint in Brad's come-to-Jesus conversion ended spectacularly one Sunday when the preacher damned to hell all those who drank alcohol, took the Lord's name in vain and committed sexual immorality. Brad had stood up, grabbed Anne and Kelsey by the arms and blundered out of the church. Kelsey paid for Brad's dramatic exodus at school. For six months, his classmates stumbled around him, bumping into walls, drooling and yelling in a crude reenactment of Brad's exit from the church. Kelsey eventually stopped beating up the kids and ignored them. Life returned to normal.

Kelsey had briefly thought about the possibility of God since his time at church, but his life was hard enough in the here and now. He didn't have the energy to consider another world outside of this one. Kelsey figured that if there was a God, he didn't care much about Kelsey or the few people he loved. Besides, Kelsey was already damned to hell for drinking, cussing and sleeping with hookers. If there was a God, he was just another asshole.

Tossing the backpack into the seat behind him, he continued to speculate. Maybe this was just another one of the books Jordyn had managed to get her hands on. Hadn't she told him she would read anything? But somehow her enjoyment of romance novels and what he knew of the Bible didn't go together.

What's more, he didn't know why it bothered him so much to see the Bible there. He didn't have anything particularly against Christian people. Was it that the Christian people he knew were so different from Jordyn and he didn't like to see her turning into one of them? Was it that he didn't want her damning him to hell the way the preacher at the church had?

It had been a long hot day and Kelsey had to resign himself to believing that this was just another of her many books. She obviously wasn't damning him. She obviously wasn't like those other church people. He took a steady breath and stared out the window until they turned into his driveway.

When they stopped in front of his house, Kelsey looked over at Jordyn. The hard line had returned around her mouth. She stared at him for a moment before remembering to smile. She leaned forward and gave him a kiss. There was no fire in her lips this night.

Kelsey reached his hand up to touch her cheek. "Are you alright, Darlin'?"

She pressed her lips together and nodded. "I just don't want to go to work, is all," she said quietly.

"Is that all?" Kelsey matched her tone and volume. He leaned his head against her forehead.

"That's all." Her breath tickled his lips.

"I'll see you in the morning then?" Kelsey asked, his voice low, his body responding to her face so close to his own.

"Mm-hm," she replied.

Their lips met again with the unquenchable fire that was becoming impossible to ignore. Their fingers twined together.

This time, she didn't pull away. Kelsey felt blood begin to beat heavily through his veins. His hand rose to touch her body, but stopped. This was not what he wanted for her. She deserved more. Maybe it was the fresh memory of the preachers condemnation of sexual immorality or something else, but Kelsey pulled away. They both drew full quavering breaths.

"I very badly want to touch you," Kelsey heard himself say. "But I—"

"Want it to be perfect?" Jordyn interrupted quietly, holding his hand in both of hers.

"Yes," Kelsey replied, surprised with how strongly he meant it. "I do want it to be perfect."

"Me too." Jordyn lifted his hand to her lips and kissed his knuckles softly. Then she held his hand, clasped in her own, against her cheek.

A full minute passed in silence before she lowered it.

"You need to get going," Kelsey said, glancing at the clock.

"I do."

"I'll pick you up for work tomorrow morning?"

"Sounds good." She shifted herself back into her seat. Kelsey noticed the firm set of her mouth. She seemed oddly determined. Writing it off as an aftereffect of their fleeting moment of passion, he stepped out of the car. He leaned his head down, hand resting on the frame of the window, and said goodbye. She blew him a kiss and drove away.

...

The thought of their kiss from the night before propelled him from bed the next morning. All apprehensions about the Bible in her backpack and her worry over Lizzie were gone with the anticipation of seeing her again. He drove too quickly to her house.

When he arrived, the Nissan wasn't in the driveway. A wave of worry and disappointment washed over him. Either she forgot they were riding together or she had not made it home last night. Both possibilities caused him to drive recklessly fast to the market. The Nissan wasn't there either.

Kelsey threw the door to the market open and asked a startled Jeannie if Jordyn had been in that morning.

"No, she's not due here for another fifteen minutes. Did you check at her house?" Jeannie's brows drew together as she spoke.

"Of course I did!" Kelsey replied, too harshly.

"Well, she should be here any moment," Jeannie replied, matching his harsh tone. "You can just learn to be patient. She doesn't need you watching her like a guard dog."

Kelsey squashed the impulse to hurl an insult at the woman and crashed out the door. His chest pounding, he drove back to Jordyn's house. As he approached, he spotted the red Nissan. His heart gave a relieved thump. His tires slid in the gravel as he came to a stop in front of her house. Jordyn was just stepping out of her car.

Kelsey flung himself out of the truck, startling her.

"Where the hell were you?" Kelsey released all the fear and anger he felt in those five words. Jordyn's eyes reflected his emotion. Kelsey noticed but was too upset to care how he was affecting her.

"I—" Jordyn began.

"I came here." Kelsey thrust a finger at the house behind her. "Then I drove to the market. You weren't there. I came back." Jordyn seemed to shrink with every word.

"If you'll let me speak..." Jordyn said quietly.

Something in the way she spoke caused Kelsey to stop. He blinked and really saw her for the first time since pulling up. She was wearing the same clothes she'd worn the night before. Her hair was roughly pulled back into a messy pile on the top of her head. Her eyes were rimmed with red and circles bloomed like bruises under them. He leaned closer to make sure she wasn't really injured. Satisfied that the circles were not bruises, he glanced over the rest of her body. She looked whole and undamaged. Her face, however, was alarming in its exhaustion.

"Jesus Christ, Jordyn. What happened?" He took an involuntary step toward her and touched her shoulder. She flinched. He brought his finger under her chin and tipped it up, searching her face. A tear rolled down her cheek and fell with a splash to the ground below.

"It was just a long night." Jordyn's eyes were pleading, begging him to let it go.

Kelsey opened his mouth to reply but found no words. Did she really expect him to believe that? Did she really expect him not to ask any more questions? Jordyn saw him searching for words and continued.

"Look, Kels, I am just really tired. I need to get cleaned up so that I can get to work." Jordyn moved to go inside. Kelsey tightened his grip on her shoulder to prevent her from going.

"Are you serious?" he asked, incredulous.

"Yes." Her chin rose defensively. "I am."

"What am I supposed to do?" Kelsey threw up his hands, not even sure what he was asking.

"You can wait here and drive me to work, or you can leave," Jordyn replied, her voice steady and defiant.

"You aren't driving yourself!"

"Wait then." With a bold look, she pulled herself from him and walked into the house. The door swung shut with a bang behind her.

Kelsey ran his hands through his hair, gathering it in his fists. He whirled on one boot and paced back and forth by his truck. Jordyn was not telling him what was going on. He didn't know how to help her or what he was supposed to do. Kelsey felt the familiar tightening of his muscles. He was ready to fight. But there was no one to fight.

Jordyn emerged from the house after ten long minutes. She kept her head down as she got in the truck. He managed to glimpse her face. She had put on some makeup to cover the circles under her eyes and brushed her hair back into a neat ponytail. She had also changed into clean clothes. Kelsey got in after her and took a deep breath before starting the truck.

"Are you ever going to tell me what is wrong?" he said as levelly as he could manage. His hand gripped the steering wheel until his knuckles turned white.

"I just can't right now, Kels," she said, her eyes focused distantly on the road and emotion vibrating through every syllable. "Just leave it. Please."

Kelsey jammed the gear shaft forward and accelerated down the road. The dust billowed behind his truck like a plume of smoke.

He would give her space for now. He would let her rest, but he would be damned to hell before he'd let her hurt in silence.

Chapter 9

IF KELSEY HAD NOT SEEN Jordyn's exhausted face that morning, he never would have known anything had happened. He picked her up from work and was met with a smile and well-rehearsed answers to all his questions. She said she hadn't felt well and didn't sleep that night. She needed to run out for milk that morning but forgot her wallet. She was upset about having to go to work again after a sleepless night. If Kelsey hadn't known Jordyn the way he did, if he had just met her, he might have believed her. Even so, it was pointless to persist. She was resolute in her story. Kelsey knew he would have to be vigilant in case it happened again. He wouldn't let her give him canned answers next time.

Although he felt unsettled about Jordyn's answers, Kelsey enjoyed every second he got to spend with her the next week. Their conversations were easy and fulfilling. Their rushed mid-drive make-out sessions left them both wanting more. They'd set aside some time to be together that weekend — outside of their cars, hopefully. He felt a frisson of excitement down his spine. He knew that this time would be important, both emotionally and physically.

Kelsey's toes tapped on the floor board of the '92 as he barreled down Highway 95 on the way to Goldfield. Steve had asked him to deliver an alternator to a customer there. It was a late-afternoon delivery and Kelsey had asked Jordyn if she wanted to accompany him. She'd said she had to pick up a shift at the market, but she was excited to see him the next day.

Kelsey would rather have had her there but daydreaming about their upcoming weekend together made the drive quick.

It was just after five o'clock when he left Steve's shop that night. It was near seven when he dropped the alternator at a shabby mobile home in the center of Goldfield, picked up a Mountain Dew and bag of potato chips at the postage stamp–sized market there and headed back down the highway. The sun was sinking lower in the sky, the heat becoming more bearable as the sun's rays passed through more atmosphere.

Kelsey imagined how Jordyn would look sitting next to him, her long legs smooth and radiant in the glow of the sun. He could see her hair blowing around her face. Her sweet lips curling into a half smile. Kelsey's thoughts were rudely interrupted by his cell phone ringing. It was his sister, Anne.

"I still can't believe you get cell phone reception out there," Anne said over the phone, her pleasant voice causing Kelsey to smile broadly.

Kelsey grunted. "No hills, I guess." His eyes scanned the desert that stretched out endlessly with only a few low-lying hills on the horizon.

"Well, I called to let you know that I got it worked out to come see you next month!" Anne spoke excitedly.

Kelsey's smile widened. "That's great, Annie!"

"Will you prep Brad for me?"

Kelsey felt a shadow pass over his face. "I will," he said shortly. "Look, I'm the one who should be visiting you."

"Just shut up about that, will you? I'm excited to come. It will be great."

Kelsey grunted in response.

"Are you still with that girl? Or did you run out of money?" Anne's teasing hit an unexpected nerve.

Kelsey bristled but was able to keep his voice easy. "You are such an asshole."

Anne giggled. "Well?" she pressed.

"Yes. I'm still with her. We have a date tomorrow, if you really want to know."

"That's great! I can't wait to... But... Have..." Anne's voice cut abruptly in and out.

Kelsey glanced at his cell phone and saw he had very little cell reception. He pulled into a driveway below a large yellow sign to see if he could regain reception.

"Anne. Annie? I lost you. Are you there?"

"Yea. I'm here. So much for having good reception." Anne laughed.

"How are things going?" Kelsey asked, putting the truck in Park and settling back in his seat.

He closed his eyes as he listened to Anne talk about her new waitressing job at the café. She enjoyed her coworkers and customers, made good tips and didn't mind the schedule. She hadn't seen her mom since he'd spoken to her last. She was making enough money to pay rent and have some left over. Kelsey's chest lightened as she spoke. He was genuinely pleased that she was doing well. He opened his eyes and focused on the yellow sign that hovered over the driveway he had parked in.

Cherry Patch Ranch.

Perfect.

He had picked a brothel to park at. He really didn't need that kind of temptation right now. He shoved the gear shaft forward and pushed down hard on the clutch.

"Hey, Annie, look, I got to get driving. Thanks for the—" Kelsey's voice cut off. His throat constricted violently and his hand froze on the shifter.

Silence hung for three seconds before Anne spoke. "Kelsey? Did I lose you again? Stupid fucking cell phones—"

"I gotta go," interrupted Kelsey loudly. He slammed the phone shut and threw it on the bench next to him. It skidded across the seat, hit the passenger door and bounced to the floor.

Kelsey's eyes were locked on a faded red Nissan Sentra parked at the Cherry Patch Ranch. His body was solid and tense as if carved from granite. The muscles around his jaw quivered. His heart beat hard and heavy.

No.

The only thought that was coherent echoed through his skull.

No. It can't be.

But Kelsey knew cars. He knew this was hers — same wheels, same body style, same trim level, same everything.

It can't be.

After a long still minute, he blinked and drew a constricted breath. He felt the familiar swell of his veins. His breath came deeper and faster. His fingertips tingled. His pupils dilated. Kelsey slammed a fist into the seat next to him.

Blinded by emotion, he pulled onto the highway. A the driver of a green Suburban swerved to miss him and honked loudly, throwing a forceful middle finger out of the driver's window. Too distracted to care that he'd narrowly missed a deadly collision, he floored it down the highway toward Beatty.

As he drove, Brad's words conjured before him, repeating themselves like a ticking engine in his mind.

Everybody says that girls a whore. She's not really my type, but I wouldn't say no.

Everybody says that girls a whore.

A whore...

He had to know.

He had to know now.

Kelsey slammed on the brakes, vaguely noting that there were no other cars on the road. He registered the smell of burning rubber and heard the squealing of tires as he cranked the steering wheel to the left and shot down the highway back toward the brothel.

He couldn't miss the flaming yellow sign lit brightly from behind by the sinking sun. Again, his tires squealed reproachfully as he turned into the driveway. He had no conscious thought of what he was going to do when he got there — he only knew that he had to have an answer. He parked next to her Nissan, almost colliding with the white picket fence that surrounded the building, and cut the engine. His stomach plummeted into his bowels as he recognized a pair of her tennis shoes laid neatly on the passenger seat of the Nissan. A fragment of his heart had held onto the possibility that it wasn't her car. He gripped his steering wheel with both hands, the leather squeaking and groaning under his palms as he wrung the worn surface.

Would he go inside? Would he wait for her? What would he do when he saw her? What would he say? What could he say?

He was spared further agonizing questions. The entrance door to the brothel opened and quickly banged shut again. His breath caught painfully in his chest. Kelsey couldn't see who came through the door and into the shadowy depths of the covered porch, but a second later, Jordyn emerged into the light, tucking a strand of hair behind her ear. She was fishing in her backpack, her face hidden from view, but he would know her anywhere. As she stepped down the first step of the deck, she glanced up. She immediately saw Kelsey's truck. A deep crease appeared on her smooth forehead, then her eyes flicked upward and locked with his. Kelsey watched the color drain from her face. She froze, maintaining eye contact. She remained as impassive and unreadable as the desert sand itself. He waited.

He watched as her chest and shoulders rose in a full breath. Then, her limbs reanimated. She broke eye contact and her lips settled into a stony expression. She carefully moved down the porch steps. Her brown hair swung loosely around her face. It was too much. Kelsey launched himself out of the truck, chest visibly vibrating from the pounding of his heart and the heaving of his breath. She didn't flinch as he slammed the door and moved around her car to face her. His arms were tensed at his sides, fists clenched. He stopped and stared at her, willing her to look at him. His chest expanded and his teeth ground together.

Look at me, god-damn you. Look at me, he thought.

She did, her eyes were steady, glinting with unreadable emotion.

"Kelsey." Her voice was quiet and husky. "What are you doing here?"

Is she really asking me that question?

"What the fuck, Jordyn?" Kelsey did not try to dampen his emotion. "What the fuck are you doing here?"

"I—I came to get my backpack." Jordyn's steady gaze faltered, though her voice remained evenly low.

Kelsey's own voice lowered to a growl. "Why the hell would your backpack be at a fucking whorehouse?" He thought he saw a moment of panic flicker through her eyes. It was gone quickly. Her mouth set in a thin line and she moved toward him, pushed past and strode purposefully around to the driver's side of her car.

"We can't do this here," Jordyn said, her voice beginning to betray the emotion that lay underneath. She unlocked the door of her car and wrenched it open, throwing her backpack inside.

"The hell we can," Kelsey said. He took two huge steps around the front of the Nissan and slammed her door shut with a powerful sweep of his arm. She jumped back from the arc of the door and glanced nervously up to the entrance of the brothel. Her eyes locked with his again.

"What do you want me to say?" she asked through clenched jaw.

"I want you to tell me what is going on here." Kelsey's teeth slammed together as he watched her face.

"I told you..."

"That you needed to get your backpack," Kelsey interrupted fiercely. "Yea. I got that part." Kelsey took a breath and felt his fingers tingling. "Why was your backpack here?"

"I— I—" she faltered, then drew herself up and continued boldly. "I left it here last weekend."

Kelsey's expression hardened, jaw muscles contracting. The silence was oppressive. She took a breath and spoke again.

"I work—" she began. "I worked here." A tear appeared in the corner of her eye and fell from her cheek into the dust below.

Kelsey slammed his fist down on the hood of her car. The noise made her blink and glance back up at the door to the brothel. "God-damn it, Jordyn! You're a hooker? What the fuck?"

Kelsey's hands went to his head. He grabbed fistfuls of hair, pushing his palms together against his pounding skull as if to hold it together. He paced in the space between their two vehicles, blindly searching the ground with his eyes.

A prostitute? They had shared so much, how could he have missed it? But it was so obvious now. Brad's words, the man called Wade in Indian Springs, the late-night shifts, last weekend when she had showed up dressed in her clothes from the night before. His insides twisted. How could he have been so stupid?

He stepped toward her, one finger raised to just inches from her face. She backed against the car, fear transforming her features for the first time. Kelsey felt the heat radiating from his body. It charged the air between them like live jumper cables. He was so close he could feel the shallow hot breaths she took. He could smell the sweet scent of her. The scent that had made him lose himself time and time again since they had met. That scent was not his anymore. He could no longer lose himself to it.

"You—" Kelsey began. "I—" He felt his voice falter as emotion more powerful than he had felt in his life drowned his words. He spoke again, mistaking anger for whatever it was that he was feeling. "I—"

I loved you, he thought desperately, finishing in his mind what he couldn't say out loud. *I loved you.*

It was the first time he had actually thought those words to himself. Thinking them to himself now, in this moment when she was no longer his to have, made his heart shatter into shards of glass. The shards tore through his chest, ripping and shredding through his innards. The physical pain made him double over. He leaned heavily onto the car frame behind her head, supporting himself with one arm. His eyes screwed shut against the pain.

"Hey!" a man's bass voice shouted from the porch. Kelsey's eyes flew open and saw panic in Jordyn's face.

"Kelsey." Her voice was pleading.

Kelsey glanced up at the porch and saw a tall brawny man dressed in a white t-shirt and jeans with cropped dark hair and black tattoos covering every inch of exposed skin. A swell of rage rushed up from the ground under Kelsey's feet, replacing the emotion he was feeling with a vengeance.

"Is this one of your men?" Kelsey looked down at Jordyn, acid dripping from his words.

"No, that's the security guy!" she said urgently. "Kelsey, you—"

"Why don't you mind your own fucking business?" Kelsey shouted at the bouncer who was now standing on the edge of the porch. Kelsey straightened but didn't move his feet. He felt rather than saw Jordyn move slightly behind him as he poised himself defensively.

"She is my business," the bouncer said, his voice low and menacing. "Step away from her now."

Kelsey realized he wanted to fight more than he ever had in his life. He started toward the porch and glared up at the well-built man standing above him. This would be good. This was what he needed.

"I said, step away from her now," the man repeated loudly.

Kelsey's eyes narrowed. "No."

The bouncer closed the space between them in a fraction of a second. Kelsey was prepared for this quick action, but didn't expect Jordyn's to interfere — before he could launch himself at the bouncer, Jordyn yelled, "No!" and grabbed his arm. That split second of time was all the bouncer needed. Kelsey saw one giant tattooed fist sailing toward his face before the world went black.

Chapter 10

A KNIFE-LIKE PAIN WAS searing a white-hot line down the front of Kelsey's forehead. Just before the pain reached his eye socket and split his eyeball in half, it stopped. It hovered over his right eyebrow, burning and throbbing. Pressing his eyelids tight, he tentatively brought a hand up to touch the spot. He half expected to feel a knife there, its point digging into his skin, but his fingers felt nothing. He pressed his palm lightly to his forehead. The pressure was soothing and dulled the pain.

He was good at waking up in strange places completely disoriented. He knew he needed to lay for a minute and think about what he remembered before opening his eyes to face his surroundings. This time, however, the headache prevented him from being able to concentrate. He was beginning to feel nervous and unsure. The surface under his body felt like it was slowly rocking back and forth. He felt seasick. He opened his left eye two millimeters and saw light blurred with indistinct pieces of furniture. He closed his eye again and the pain dug deeper.

Fingertips brushed over the hand he had placed on his forehead, soft but lingering.

"Do you need some water?" a woman's voice spoke directly over his face. Kelsey could feel warm breath tickle his cheeks.

Jordyn.

A surge of nausea that had nothing to do with his splitting headache made him turn onto his side, instinctively aiming for a place to vomit. Nothing came up and the movement caused the knife in his skull to cut with a renewed vengeance. He brought the other hand up to cover his eyes. The darkness helped and after a few deep breaths, the pain dulled again.

"Here, if you can drink, take this aspirin." Her hand was on his arm, pressing lightly, insistent.

He wanted to pretend Jordyn wasn't there, to ignore her, but the pain made his decision for him. He half opened his eye again and saw a hand holding a glass of water just inches from his face. He clumsily propped himself up on one elbow, grabbed the glass of water and pills that were offered and gulped them both down. Water dribbled down his cheek and soaked the soft surface under him. He fell back down on his shoulder, letting the cool water soothe his throat. Gradually the pain lessened. He drifted off to sleep in relieved exhaustion.

The sound of a closing door woke him. He was disoriented, but the pain in his head lessened and he was able to concentrate, to remember his last moments of consciousness. As that memory returned, so did the nausea. He let himself fall back onto the bed, which was overly soft and covered in a quilted blanket. He peeked under his heavy, swollen eyelids. He was in a sparsely furnished bedroom with a dark laminate dresser and bedframe. Thick maroon curtains concealed a window that appeared to look out on a dark night. A shiny brass lamp standing in the corner next to a closed door cast its yellow light onto a faded blue recliner. In the recliner sat Jordyn. He closed his eyes again.

"Where am I?" Kelsey asked, his voice thick as motor oil in his throat. He heard Jordyn shift, but didn't feel her come nearer.

"My boss's— My old boss's private quarters." Jordyn's voice sounded thick as well. When Kelsey didn't respond, she continued, "I just explained to her that you were my...my friend. She let me bring you in here." Kelsey winced at the words 'my friend'. He heard her stand up and move closer but she didn't touch him. "Kels, I think Devin broke your nose." Her voice faltered.

"I'm still at the brothel?" Kelsey ignored the fact that his nose was broken. The anger was beginning to beat through his veins again. He opened his eyes, keeping them fixed on the yellowed drop-tile ceiling above him. "Did you put me in one of...one of the rooms?" He swallowed back the bitter taste in the back of his throat. His chest began to rise and fall more rapidly. "God, Jordyn, how many men have you fucked in this room?" His hands flew up to his forehead and his fingers dug into his hair. His eyes flicked back and forth, searching the ceiling for sanity.

His heated questions went unanswered for a long minute. He heard her sit back down in the recliner. When she spoke, her voice was broken but firm. "Kelsey Campbell, I deserve every bit of your anger. But I can't talk to you when you are so angry. For one thing, if Devin hears you yelling he'll come in here and break some other part of your body. So, I'll answer your questions, you deserve that, but I'll only talk when you can listen."

Her words caught Kelsey off guard. He had been ready for a fight. He became aware of the rapid rise and fall of his chest, his tight muscles and the hard set of his jaw. If he wanted answers, he was going to have to rein it in. Did he want answers? Did he really want to know the details? But, wasn't that why he'd come back to the brothel in the first place? As much as he didn't want to know, he had to. He had loved her. He still loved her. With great effort, he loosened his jaw.

Jordyn remained silent and still while Kelsey attempted to regain control of himself. After ten long minutes, he took a steady breath and spoke, "Go ahead." He rested his hands on his chest in what he hoped was an unthreatening position. He focused on taking deep breaths as she began to talk.

"I started working here when I was 18." Her voice was quiet and quavering. Kelsey did the math quickly. Three years. "I was done with high school and had just got the job at the market. It didn't pay enough to give Lizzie what she deserves." Jordyn's voice broke and he heard her take a shaky breath. "Leeta came into the market one day." She paused. "Leeta's the owner of this place. This is her room." Jordyn paused again and took in a deep breath. "I don't even remember how we started talking about the brothel. But we got along really well and I came to work for her.

"I made more money in one night than I did all week at the market. I'd never seen cash like that before. I used it to buy Lizzie new clothes, take her out to eat and pay for her doctor's bills.

"I didn't like the work like some of the other girls though. I had to sort of turn off my brain, if that makes any sense. I convinced myself that doing a job I didn't like was a small price to pay if it made a difference in Lizzie's life."

Jordyn paused. Was she waiting for him to say something? Kelsey couldn't speak. His jaw muscles were vice tight. His heart threatened to thud out of his chest. Somehow he managed to keep his breath slow and steady.

She repositioned herself on the recliner before she continued. Her voice was stronger and pleading. "Kelsey, I want you to know that I came here to quit tonight. You gave me a glimpse of what love could be. I'd read about love, but you showed it to me. I can't continue to work and lose that glimmer of hope."

Kelsey turned his head toward Jordyn and looked at her in the eyes for the first time since he'd woken up in the strange room. Her eyes were bright with tears. She was leaning forward, her hands twisting in her lap. She saw the question in his eyes.

Why?

"It was Lizzie's doctor visit. Her heart screenings. I wanted to be able to take her shopping and go out to eat like we always did. I..." She stopped and buried her face in her hands. Her shoulders shook though she remained silent. After a minute she raised her face, tears streaming from reddened eyes. "After our first date, I knew I couldn't continue whoring after my first client showed up..."

At those words, something inside Kelsey burst. He couldn't lay there anymore. Though it cost him to move, he pushed himself upright and swung his legs around. Jordyn started and looked at him warily. His head throbbed for a few beats before mercifully dulling.

Jordyn's tormented voice continued, "It was a mistake, Kelsey. I knew it right—"

"Do you have a cigarette?" Kelsey interrupted her brusquely.

"Uh, yea." Jordyn jumped up and looked around the room. She picked up her backpack then, glancing nervously at him, came close and set the bag at the foot of the bed. She fumbled for a while and finally drew out a pack with one cigarette left in it and a neon green lighter. With trembling hands, she held them out to Kelsey. "I'm sorry, since I quit smoking...I only have one..."

Kelsey held up a hand to interrupt her again. "Just stop. Give me a minute okay?" Kelsey felt a twinge of regret at the hurt in her eyes. She dropped her gaze as Kelsey lit the cigarette and inhaled. He held his breath until his lungs burned before blowing slowly out. The smoke curled into his nostrils and fogged his vision.

"What I can't believe... What just kills me," Kelsey said thoughtfully into the smoky cloud surrounding him, "is that I tried so hard to respect you. I tried so hard to make our time together perfect." He took a long drag on the cigarette. "But this whole time, I could've just come over here and paid to fuck you like the rest of the god-damn world." He heard a stifled sob next to him but didn't turn to face her. "I can't believe I didn't see it. That little shit, Wade, in Indian Springs knew it." Kelsey paused, cocking his head to the side. "Was he one of your 'clients'?" Kelsey lingered contemptuously on the word 'client'. An agonized sob came from the end of the bed.

"Yea. I thought so." Kelsey looked at the half-smoked cigarette in his hand, watching the smoldering tip. He tapped it with one long finger and the ashes floated to the carpeted floor.

Jordyn was crying in earnest now. Kelsey finished his cigarette while he listened to her. Earlier in the day, the sound of her crying would have sent him flying to her side. He would have done anything to make it stop; but now, he felt numb.

Jordyn's crying faded to an occasional sniff. Kelsey turned his head to face her. Her hands were in her lap and eyes downcast. At his movement though, she turned her eyes up to meet his. The torture he saw there felt like a physical blow to his stomach. He couldn't hold her gaze. He glanced down. The backpack on the bed had tipped and spilled its contents. He felt a caustic burst of laughter leave his chest. Her eyes flicked from his face to the bed, alarmed.

"That's ironic isn't it?" Kelsey said in answer to her confusion. She frowned. He continued, "A hooker with a Bible?" Jordyn's mouth fell open slightly and her eyes narrowed. Again, he answered her unasked question. "I saw it in there the other day when I got your water bottle out of that backpack." Kelsey turned his face away from her, the backpack and the leatherbound Bible peaking from inside it. "Just funny that you carry that thing around with you, being a whore and all." He ignored the sharp intake of breath next to him.

The silence didn't linger this time. Jordyn spoke, her voice steady, "Is it though?"

"What?" Kelsey shot back at her, turning to look at her and raising an eyebrow.

"I mean," Jordyn continued levelly, "is it ironic to have a...a whore reading a Bible?" Her voice caught. "Everyone in that book is a bunch of horrible people doing horrible things to each other and God. Seems like a whore is a perfect person to be reading about that shit." Her voice grew slightly stronger. "Seems like that's the whole point of it. People do a bunch of shitty stuff and Jesus shows up to fix everything."

"You know what, Jordyn? I really don't want to be preached at right now. Especially by you." He glanced at her face as he spoke and caught the agony his words caused. Again, he felt the pang of regret. His insides twisted as she looked quickly back to her lap.

"I know," she said quietly. "I'm sorry. I'm the worst."

"That's just the thing though, isn't it?" Kelsey pressed the cooled cigarette butt into the top of his knee, grinding the ashes into the fabric of his jeans. "I'm just the same." He felt her gaze penetrate the side of his head. "At least you make money having sex with dudes. I always have to pay the girls I'm with." He looked into her eyes, knowing that his face was blank.

"What are you saying, Kelsey?" she asked slowly.

"I'm saying that I frequently enjoy the company of whores." A mirthless laugh followed his confession. "But, unlike you, I haven't been to see one of the girls since our first date." The words were acid in his mouth.

Silent tears brimmed in her eyes and cascaded down her cheeks. Her eyes were wide and fixed on his face. Kelsey laughed short and humorlessly. Pain twisted through her features, mixed with something else. Was it pity?

"I can't do this." Kelsey pushed himself to his feet, ignoring the pounding in his head. Briefly looking around for his keys, he remembered he'd left them in his truck. Jordyn stood.

"Kelsey." The sound of her pleading voice saying his name propelled him forward and out the door next to the lamp. He blindly fumbled his way through the new room he entered, out the front door and down a set of shallow steps. His truck was parked a hundred yards away, lit dimly by murky porchlight. He staggered through the moonless night toward it.

As the truck started roughly and Kelsey backed out of his parking spot, he noted that Jordyn had not followed him.

Good, he thought grimly. *Hopefully she forgets I exist.*

He drove as reckless as his emotions toward the only comfort he could think of — the comfort freshest on his mind because of her. How could he not think of visiting his Angels now? He'd just lost the only thing that filled that void in his life. With the Angels, there were no strings attached and no reason to do things perfectly. The pink lights loomed ahead, filled with the promise of oblivion, bought and paid for.

The thick wood door of the brothel barely swung shut when Kelsey spotted Charity. She was leaning against the bar talking with one of the other girls. He crossed the room in two strides and smiled as he put his hands on her waist to pull her in for a kiss. When he had his fill and let go, she giggled.

"Well, Kelsey, I don't know what to say!" she said in mock indignation. Then she reached up and touched his cheek, frowning slightly. "What did you do to your face? Is your nose broken?" Kelsey waved her hand away, dismissing her concern. He buried his face in her neck and she giggled again.

He was normally drunk when he was here. Her skin was delightful when he had all his faculties. He had to remember to come sober more often.

"Say you'll take me to bed with you," Kelsey breathed into her soft skin.

The change in her eyes was instant. Her mouth softened and her eyes sparkled. She blinked and pressed her body against his. He was aware of every curve. She reached on tiptoes to whisper in his ear; her low voice tickled the hair around his cheekbone. "Come to bed with me."

Without another word, she led him down the hall and into a room lit by a single lamp. She backed in, maintaining eye contact, and began to strip off her clothes. Each piece fell to the floor and revealed more of her perfectly shaped body: shoulders, breasts, waist, hips. Kelsey watched her, waiting for his body to respond before he took his own clothes off. When she was completely naked, she walked slowly forward, allowing him a full view of her body. She put her hands on his chest.

"Here, let me help you," she said as she slid her hands under his shirt and pulled it over his head. The skin on his chest tingled as she touched it. She moved her hands down to work on his pants, but he took a step back.

"Hold on," he said. "Give me a minute."

She looked into his face and a sly smile stretched her lips. "Oh, I think I can help with that too," she said and grabbed his hand. She led him over to the bed and pushed him playfully onto the plush gold comforter. The bed groaned softly as he sat down. She knelt before him, running her hands up his thighs.

Kelsey watched her, feeling disoriented, his head still pounding. It was as if he was sitting outside of his own self, watching in clinical interest. His body, usually ready before he stepped a toe into the brothel, felt numb and distant. As Charity looked up into his eyes and resumed working at the button of his jeans, he felt his eyebrows draw together. Charity's seductive face flickered for a moment before she bent to kiss his chest.

He watched her platinum blond hair fall across his torso as she trailed kisses over his chest and belly. Kelsey saw his own hand rise up and push her head back a bit. Her eyes met his again, questioning this time. He put his finger under her chin and lifted her face so that the lamp lit it fully. Her hands stopped their ministrations and a line formed between her eyebrows. He could see she was working to retain her flirtatious smile.

Kelsey studied her face. Makeup hid most of her bare skin, but he saw a hint of darkness under her eyes. He saw that her long dark eyelashes were fake. One of them was starting to come off. Her lips were painted a bright pink tonight. He had a wild impulse to wipe away the lipstick. He glanced up through her hair and noticed that the platinum blond was beginning to grow out, revealing a thin dark line of coffee brown hair at the roots. Her painted smile flickered. She moved a fraction away from him but he kept his finger firmly under her chin.

He was asking her silent questions, his eyes examining her features.

Do you have a sister with Down syndrome? Are you here tonight to pay for your sister's doctor's bills? Do you have a crack-head mother and a nonexistent father? Do you have someone you love who doesn't know you are here? Do you have a Bible lying hidden in your bag?

Kelsey heard himself speak, his tone conversational, "Do you like working here?"

A real look of alarm passed over Charity. She stood and backed away from him, grabbing her clothes from the floor as she did. She gathered them to her breasts.

"What is wrong with you tonight?" Her voice was angry, not at all like what he'd heard from her before. "You get out of here before I call Nick in." She pointed out the door. "Get out."

Kelsey felt himself stand up. He nodded at Charity, who pursed her lips and scowled at him. He swept his wrinkled shirt from the floor and left the room. Still shirtless, he walked by the bar, out the door and into the dark parking lot.

The throbbing pain from being punched earlier had not left his head; and now, his vision was beginning to blur. Nausea filled his belly. Just as he sat in his truck, the earth tipped over under him. For the second time in twenty-four hours, the world went black.

Chapter 11

THE INSIDE OF KELSEY'S eyelids were glowing red and his body hot and damp with sweat. The searing pain from his head was gone and replaced by slight dizziness. He cracked an eye open and immediately slammed it shut again as the bright sunlight threatened to burst his pupils. He sat still, eyes closed, until the heat in the cab of his truck caused the sweat to trickle from his temples and roll down the small of his back. He squirmed on the seat. Opening his eyes as little as possible, he fumbled around for his keys before finding them wedged behind him. Soon, the truck roared to life and spewed dusty hot air from the vents. Kelsey coughed, forced his eyes wider in order to see the parking lot and maneuver the truck onto the highway.

Brad was reclined in his chair, smoking a cigarette and watching a cops television show in their heavily curtained living room when Kelsey slammed the door shut behind him. Brad stirred.

"You're up early for Saturday morning." Brad's voice was gravelly, probably the first words he'd spoken all day. He glanced back at Kelsey. "Or home late." He grunted. "Did you give the Angels a good one for me?" Brad laughed joylessly at himself as Kelsey's stomach turned over. Kelsey managed to keep the nausea at bay and stumbled half blindly into his room.

Sleep was the only true escape from the internal turmoil Kelsey felt; and, graciously, sleep is what his body demanded. He fell onto his bed and slept until the sound of a truck revving to life outside woke him. He reached up to gingerly touch his face. He sucked in a small breath as he probed his tender swollen nose. Dried blood was flaked into his hair.

The waves of pain from his nose and hungry cramping belly were nothing compared to the tsunami of loss that threatened to drown him alive. The full weight of what had happened the night before washed over him. He was adrift; lying there staring at the ceiling did nothing to settle him.

The smell of dried blood and rancid sweat was added to the nausea. After a few long minutes, he reluctantly heaved himself upright and went to shower. The steaming trickles of water cascaded down his body. It revived him and he felt the return of his focus. With the return of focus came a flood of more memories, as sharp and painful as the water that shot at a boiling temperature from the shower head. Charity's body pressed seductively against his knees, hands working insistently at the button of his jeans. Her painted eyes looking into his own, plastered with the expression that she'd used for so many men.

Charity was never more to me than a hired hand to stroke my ego and my dick, he thought. *It was always a lie.*

Any passion she had felt for him had been an illusion, and he had chosen to believe this lie with reckless fury. The vision of Charity loomed in front of him; she was screaming at him, clothes clutched to her naked breasts. Charity's face began to mutate and Jordyn's took its place. Now Jordyn was screaming at him, her face contorted in so much anger it was nearly unrecognizable. Kelsey squeezed his eyes shut and turned the water to cold. The freezing water made his skin ripple into goose flesh. Every hair on his body stood on end. His breath caught in his chest. Still, Kelsey could see her face, hear her angry words, feel his soul being torn top to bottom. He ripped open the shower curtain and flicked the water off. He stood, chest heaving and water dripping onto the floor in a puddle around his feet.

Not only had Jordyn been taken from him, but apparently any enjoyment of another woman was lost as well.

You can't lose what you never had, he thought bitterly.

An odd bubble rose inside of his chest. It moved through his throat and came out of his mouth in a strangled moan. Before he could understand what was happening to him, his shoulders began to shake and his eyes began to swell. Tears rolled warm and soothing down his cheeks. They fell to the ground and washed away what the shower could not. His heart became as fluid as his tears, pooling in his chest. By the time the tears stopped falling, he felt as vulnerable as a child.

It was late afternoon as he sat at the kitchen table, soothing his dry throat with a glass of water. Brad was gone. The house was quiet. In the silence, he felt a sharp pang of loss when he remembered that he was supposed to have had the entire day alone with Jordyn: alone with his Darlin', making things perfect.

The thought of their lost weekend and what might have been propelled him from his seat at the kitchen table. The wobbly wooden chair scraped heavily on the linoleum and nearly tipped over. Kelsey grabbed a handful of his wet tussled hair and leaned his head against his fist. He began to pace around the table. The vulnerability left from his tears in the bathroom was being replaced by a sense of urgency and action.

His life and their relationship were a mess — too much had been said, too much had been done. Could he risk seeing her again? Did he need to leave town? Could he bear to be away from her?

He wondered what she was doing now. Terrible visions of who she could be doing flashed through his scattered mind. His fists clenched and he slammed them into the table, splitting the tops of three knuckles. He leaned over the table, breathing heavily.

But how could he judge her? He was doing the same thing, and wasn't he worse? He wasn't trying to support a druggy mom and disabled sister by sleeping with the Angels, just satisfying his own body's desires.

But how could they ever see each other without thinking of what the other had done? This question seeped like acid through his core. He couldn't see a way to make it work. Much stronger people had ended their relationships for much less. He had to face it, this was the end.

Another smear of blood stained the table where his knuckles drove into it. His mind continued to reel. If it was the end, why couldn't he let it go? Why did he still feel like there was a way? Could he dare to believe she would see him again?

The front door slammed shut and startled Kelsey upright. Brad flung his keys onto the kitchen table, opened the refrigerator and shoved two six-packs of Coors inside. Grabbing two of the Coors with one hand, Brad popped the tops off both on the kitchen counter. Ignoring his son, he ambled back in the living room. Ten seconds later the garbled bellows of the television filled the house.

With the mess his thoughts were, Kelsey knew he couldn't be home with Brad right now. He bolted out the door, nearly forgetting his keys.

He knew where he was going to go before he had even entered his truck; but he didn't let himself think about it, otherwise he would stop. He would realize the stupidity of what he was doing. He would realize the improbability of her letting him get within 100 yards of her house.

When he cut the engine in front of her mobile home, he knew he should turn it back on and drive away. Showing up here was cruel, maybe even abusive. But he could feel her close. And he had already lost everything.

Lizzie answered the door, catching Kelsey off guard. His muscles had been tensed, ready to push his already bloodied hand between the jam and the door if Jordyn tried to slam it in his face. Lizzie's trusting eyes looked into his and drained the tension from him.

"Hi, Kelsey." Lizzie's simple greeting was filled with sweetness and soothed his hammering heart.

"H-Hi, Lizzie." There was a pause that felt too long to Kelsey, but Lizzie smiled serenely at him. "How are you?" he asked lamely.

"Good," she replied. "Do you want to watch a Discovery Channel show with me?"

Kelsey's words caught in his throat and his mouth opened. He was disarmed.

"I think he's here to see me, Lizzie Girl." Jordyn's quiet voice hit him like a sledge hammer to the chest and restarted his heart pounding in his ears.

She stood with one hand against the wall that led down the hall. Her eyes were fixed on Lizzie, gentle and filled with love for her sister. His heart somersaulted at the tenderness in her face. Kelsey was glad she didn't look at him. He didn't want her to lose that expression. Lizzie, defeated, plopped down on the couch.

Jordyn spoke again, "We'll just be in my room if you need us, Lizzie."

"Okay," Lizzie replied and focused her attention on the television.

Without looking in his direction, Jordyn turned and walked down the hallway to her room. Kelsey eventually decided to follow her. She had told Lizzie they'd be in her room after all. He walked toward her room, wondering why he seemed to be tiptoeing. As his arm stretched to push open her door, he noticed his hand was trembling. He took a deep breath and stepped inside.

Jordyn stood on the far side of the room, leaning against her desk. Her hands gripped the wooden edge, knuckles white, and her eyes stared fixedly on the floor, partially hiding her face from view. Kelsey's immediate reaction was to cross the floor in one step and pull her into him. He wanted to bury his face into her smooth hair and feel her warmth next to him. Only his fingers twitched in response to this urge. His body was stone. He couldn't do that now. Although she was only ten feet away, she was as unreachable to him as if she stood on another continent. His gaze fell to the floor.

Time slowed and maybe stopped. The only sounds were small intakes of breath that might've been from either of them: small moments in a void of time when words weren't enough. The silence was like another person in the room, speaking for them and saying it all.

The impossibility of talking became a weight too heavy for Kelsey to bear. Why had he come? There was nothing that could be said. Judging from her silence, she felt the same.

Leave now, Kelsey, while you still have some dignity.

His fingers twitched again.

"Don't do it."

The words were a breath. He thought he had imagined them. His fingers twitched again.

"Don't go."

He was sure she'd spoken this time. His eyes flicked to her face at the same time that she looked up at him. Their eyes locked for a moment before they both looked away.

"There's nothing to say, Jordyn." Kelsey spoke without breath. His words melted into the hungry silence around them.

"Like hell there's nothing to say." Jordyn's voice was still quiet but sparked with familiar defiance. Kelsey looked at her in surprise.

She was focused on him, face unreadable.

"You wouldn't have come if there was nothing to say," she said steadily. "And I wouldn't have been waiting for you all day either."

Kelsey's heart gave a great thump. *She was waiting for me.*

Suddenly, Kelsey's body was too heavy to hold upright. He sat solidly on the bed. It creaked and bounced under his weight. He let his elbows rest on his knees, head in his hands. He let out a slow breath.

"We can't fix this thing, Jordyn. I've hurt you too much. You...you've..." Kelsey choked on his words.

"I've hurt you too much," Jordyn finished for him.

Another slow breath, and another. The silence spoke again, louder than their own voices.

His elbows dug into the top of his knees in painful points and his face was damp with sweat from his hands before the bed softly creaked and bounced next to him. He felt her body next to him as sure as if he was embracing her. The space between them was like another person in the room. It was getting crowded.

The door opened and Lizzie's face popped in, shocking them both upright.

"I'm going to bed," Lizzie said with a yawn. Kelsey glanced outside. The sky was dark. How long had he been there?

Jordyn cleared her throat. "Okay. Remember to brush your teeth."

"Yes." Lizzie rubbed her eyes.

"I love you, Lizzie Girl," Jordyn said softly, a smile in her voice.

"I love you too. I love you too, Kelsey," Lizzie said as she turned to walk down the hall, long brown hair swinging behind her. Kelsey choked on his words again.

The silence returned but only for a moment.

"I went to the brothel last night." Kelsey's own voice startled him.

That is the first fucking thing you chose to say to her? He frowned into his hands.

"Okay..." she said. Kelsey thought he heard her voice quaver.

Something about her emotion emboldened him. "I went there after I left you."

He felt her weight shift on the bed as she spoke, "What do you want me to s—"

"I couldn't go through with it," Kelsey interrupted her. "I'd seen this girl many times before, but I couldn't do it." He heard a muffled sob and saw her shoulders shake in his peripheral vision. "I couldn't do it...because of you," Kelsey continued, voice still strong. "Because I...because I love you."

The words drove away the silence and filled the space between them, wrapping them in a tangible presence. The words waited there patiently and peacefully.

"I love you too, Kels."

Jordyn's words joined Kelsey's and twined together, leaving an indelible mark on their hearts.

Kelsey drew a short wavering breath. His chest expanded with hope and deflated again in defeat. Love was *not* enough. It hadn't been enough for his mom. It hadn't been enough for his step-mom. All that awaited love was heartbreak and death. If either of those didn't destroy it then drugs, alcohol, sex or any number of other things would. Love was never enough.

"Can we let love be enough?" Jordyn spoke quietly next to him. It took a second to register what she'd said. Her words were in direct contrast to his thoughts.

"What?" he asked, more to give himself time to process than because he hadn't heard.

"Can't we let love be enough to fix it all?" Jordyn repeated, stronger this time.

"Jordyn, I—" Kelsey couldn't finish what he wanted to say. He couldn't tell her that their love couldn't be enough.

"I've read that true love doesn't keep a record of wrongs. I've read that it always trusts, hopes and endures." Jordyn took a breath to continue. "You and I don't have good examples of that in our lives, Kels. Both sets of parents are a mess. But I think that the love I feel for Lizzie or you for Anne resemble true love. Because of them, I believe it's possible. So can we try?" A tentative hand reached out to touch his knee. Its soft weight sent shivers up Kelsey's spine. "Can we let it be possible?"

The silence returned, quieter this time, muffled by their spoken words. He wanted to say yes. He wanted to jump in with both feet and wild abandon, but the pain of the night before was too fresh. The wounds still bled freely.

He couldn't jump all in, but could he agree to trying? Could he agree to exploring the possibility that love could really be enough? He wanted to laugh out loud at the absurdity. The insistent weight of her hand on his knee held him back from laughter. This was a hand that should not be there. He'd hurt the woman attached to that hand more than any other person in his life. Yet, there she was, against all odds, asking for him to try.

Kelsey's shoulders slumped. A thousand words ran through his mind. He heard himself speak, "I can't let it be enough right now. I can't give you what you want. I'll stick around but I'm going to need time."

Her fingers tightened on his knee. Kelsey turned his face toward hers and really looked at her for the first time that evening. Her eyes were lined and her cheeks streaked with tears. Her face was pale from fatigue. Her body slumped, struggling to hold upright. Behind the exhaustion, however, her eyes sparked. The corners of her mouth were soft and turned upward. Her fingers gripped into his knee, holding him. She was vibrating with unmistakable, impossible hope. He felt his heart lighten. The unstaunched bleeding that was draining him of life slowed and he felt his face soften to match hers.

Chapter 12

EARLY MORNING LIGHT diffused over the desert as Kelsey and Jordyn lay on her bed, looking out the window. The clothes that they'd worn since the day before felt fused to their bodies and Kelsey's tennis shoes gripped uncomfortably on his feet. Despite being desperately hungry and in need of a long nap, neither one of them wanted to move. Jordyn's head nestled tightly against his shoulder. Her hand rested on the center of his chest, playing idly with the collar of his t-shirt. His breathing lightly ruffled her hair and it tickled his chin.

"This isn't exactly how I pictured spending our first night alone together," Kelsey said into the growing light of the room. His voice was gravelly from not having spoken for hours.

"I know," Jordyn said. Her voice sent soothing vibrations through his shoulder. "Me either."

The sky grew bright orange on the horizon. The darkness retreated across the sky leaving a lavender stain in its wake. A small dirty-brown bird lit on the branch of a sage bush and perched sentinel over the dusty earth. A diesel truck engine started up outside. The world was coming alive.

"Now what?" Kelsey asked. They both knew that question couldn't ultimately be answered. They lay in silence for a few more moments.

"How about breakfast?" Jordyn finally said.

Kelsey took a steadying breath and stroked her hair back from her cheek. "That sounds like a start."

Jordyn pushed herself upright, her comforting weight against his side disappearing and a cool emptiness replacing it. He blinked up at her face and propped himself up on his elbows. She was biting her lip and studying the ceiling. The physical emptiness he felt from losing her body next to his was echoed in her face.

"What is it, Darlin'?" Kelsey asked. Judging from the look on her face, he wasn't sure if he wanted to know the answer.

The moment stretched long between them. Her eyes continued to search the ceiling while the rest of her was still. Kelsey's chest felt heavy as he watched her. She took in a deep shuddering breath. Kelsey felt his forehead crease.

Her words came fast, tripping over each other. "Can we run away together sometime? For the weekend, I mean."

Kelsey held his breath as he replied, "Yes…"

She nodded, looking into her lap.

Kelsey squinted at her. "Is that all?"

She glanced at him, her eyes guarded. "For now."

…

Fuck. She has been crying.

Kelsey smashed the red button on his cell phone and shoved it into his pocket. She had tried to sound normal, but there was unmistakable emotion in her voice.

Kelsey grabbed the half-empty pack of cigarettes and a lighter from the kitchen counter. The smoke curled around his ears as he exhaled slowly, contemplating. She said she would be here in about an hour. She hadn't said why she was coming. Technically, she didn't need a reason to visit, but something was wrong.

It had been a week since their all-night conversation — a bittersweet week. Kelsey wondered why she had decided to give him time. He often wondered if he should end it, but he was too weak.

He loved having her near him on their carpools to and from work. Their conversation was easy, their physical chemistry undeniable. Despite outward appearances, there were moments that cut him quick and deep; moments when he would look at her and see the young prostitute she had been; moments when the men she had been with paraded in front of his vision, leering at him with a knowing look; moments when he felt Charity's thighs on his own, her naked breasts pressed to his bare chest; moments when the mess of his life became unbearable.

If Jordyn was experiencing what he was, he could definitely see why she might've been crying. But during the week, she hadn't given him any indication of internal struggle. Obviously, something had changed. Now Kelsey figured he was going to spend his Friday night figuring out what that was.

He smashed his spent cigarette out in the ash tray on the kitchen table. A thump and slow movement down the hall alerted Kelsey that Brad had finally decided to get up for the day. Kelsey looked at his black Casio watch — 4:30 pm. He rolled his eyes.

"Must be nice not having to work," Kelsey shot down the hall, knowing it would irritate Brad.

"Fuck off," came the half-hearted blundering response. Brad came into the light of the kitchen, gym shorts hanging low under his blotchy, distended belly. He scratched his stubbled cheek. "Must be nice having a back that isn't shit," he spat at Kelsey and headed for the refrigerator.

Kelsey leaned against the kitchen counter and watched Brad prepare a bowl of cereal for himself. His father was painful to watch. The alcohol that perpetually flowed through his veins made him shaky and clumsy. His eyes were unfocused and his body seemed to work apart from his brain. Ironically, the more he drank, the better his focus was — especially when he drank whiskey. Kelsey shuddered, pushing away the memories of his and Anne's mothers.

Anne.

"Anne's coming to town soon," Kelsey said, not expecting any response.

To his surprise, Brad straightened and made eye contact with Kelsey. Kelsey hadn't looked into Brad's eyes in any recent memory. He resisted the urge to look away. Brad's eyes were slightly yellowed and the brown iris' faded into muddy grey. Normally dull and lifeless, a spark shone behind them at the mention of his sister. Kelsey didn't like it.

"Oh? When?" Brad asked, still maintaining eye contact. Kelsey reached for another cigarette as an excuse to look away. He flicked the lighter on.

"I don't know. A month, maybe?" He inhaled, filling his lungs with smoke, and looked out the window. He felt Brad's gaze on the side of his head.

"That girl always looked so much like her mother." Brad paused. Kelsey could hear Brad's thoughts tumbling like sage brush in the wind. "Her mother coming with her?"

Kelsey snorted. "Why the fuck would she bring that druggy with her?"

Brad slammed the milk jug he was holding down on the counter, the liquid sloshing out of the open top and splattering onto the floor. Kelsey was used to these minor displays of aggression and didn't flinch.

"You watch your mouth when you talk about my Delilah," Brad spit at him.

"Your Delilah?" Kelsey drawled. "Since when do you give a fuck about her?"

Brad took a step closer but stayed out of Kelsey's reach.

"I said, watch your mouth." Brad's voice lowered and the tips of his teeth showed.

Kelsey took a drag on the cigarette and blew it toward the window.

Brad grabbed the milk jug again, squeezing the plastic handle until it made a popping sound. "That woman is mine. Always has been and always will, until the day she dies."

Kelsey laughed shortly. "I think you mean until the day you die, Pops."

The milk jug flew toward Kelsey's head and he ducked with enough time to watch it land with a heavy slap. Milk glugged lazily onto the floor.

Kelsey grinned at his father who stood red-faced and seething. Sucking in another long drag, he rubbed his cigarette out in the ash tray. As he casually watched the ashes smolder, Brad hurled his body toward Kelsey. The force of their collision sent a bolt of adrenaline coursing through Kelsey's veins. Brad pulled his arm back and aimed a closed fist at Kelsey's jaw. But Brad was clumsy and Kelsey was quick. Kelsey dodged the misaimed blow. He wrapped Brad's neck in a tight hug with his bicep and forearm and brought his closed fist into the soft flab of Brad's belly. Brad grunted and drool splattered on the floor below him.

Kelsey brought his lips close to Brad's ear and spoke in a whisper. "Better luck next time old man."

Kelsey released his father, leaving Brad doubled over and panting. Kelsey turned on his heel and walked down the hall.

...

It was late in the afternoon when Kelsey heard her Nissan in the driveway. He smiled when he saw her black and white sneakers slide out of the car and onto the dirt. She stood tall, pushing her arms into the sky in a slow stretch that showed off the sheer length of her. She was all long legs and arms. Her flowy white t-shirt came up to reveal a perfect round belly button playing peek-a-boo above a pair of cutoff blue jean shorts. She stood on tip toes, then dropped her arms next to her body. Her gaze searched the trailer and found him watching her through the window. Her full mouth stretched into a wide smile. Suddenly the smoky confines of the trailer were too much. He had to be next to her.

In his haste he bumped the table by Brad's ratty recliner, knocking over a half-full bottle of warm beer onto the floor. Not bothering to pick it up, he crossed the space of the living room in one long step. With a whoosh of hot air, he crashed the front door open and bounded down the front steps. He took the last few feet of distance between them in another long stride, pushed her car door shut with a thud and grabbed her around the waist. He lifted her up onto her toes as he hugged her close. Her hair smelled like floral shampoo, her skin felt smooth and he buried his head into her neck, breathing her in like she was his last breath. She giggled as he nuzzled her neck, sending small tickling vibrations through his t-shirt to his chest. He felt her breath on his chest, warm then cool as she breathed in and out. They stood there, unmoving, and Kelsey forgot the tears he'd heard in her voice on the phone earlier.

Finally, she pulled back and looked up at him. Her pale green eyes were glittering with a mix of emotion unfamiliar to him. Was it happiness to see him, or something else? She seemed happy enough, white teeth showing in a broad smile behind her petal pink lips. She held onto his biceps, her soft hands pressing firmly into his skin. He searched her face, pulling her back to appraise the rest of her, making sure she wasn't hurt. She squeezed his arms and smiled bigger.

"How are you doing, Darlin'?" he asked, and watched as her cheeks flushed a lovely shade of pink. He smiled and kissed both of the pink splotches as they spread toward her ears.

"So good, now that I'm with you," she answered with a smile that made her ears stick out a little more. As she smiled, another flash of unfamiliar emotion crossed her face and she looked away, toward her car.

Kelsey bent to look her in the face, squeezing her shoulders. "Hey," he said, "Jordyn, Darlin', what's the matter?"

She glanced up at him, not holding his gaze. "I...just..." She trailed off. In a flurry of movement, she opened the back door of her car and waved inside.

Kelsey looked inside at the two brown sleeping bags rolled tightly and tied with a strand of twine. They sat on top of two pillows covered with old striped pillow cases. Her ancient backpack, stuffed full, sat on the back seat. A small red and white cooler was wedged behind the driver's side seat. A large lumpy-looking bundle lay on the floor with a pair of tennis shoes and a light jacket. He looked at Jordyn, alarm in his eyes.

"Are you leaving?" His mouth dried as he spoke.

She paused, then smiled shyly, her hand resting on the open car door. "Only if you come with me."

It didn't take him more than a few seconds to make his decision. Before he bothered to ask any logistical questions like where they were going, for how long and how they were going to pay for it, he kissed her full mouth and said, "Of course I'm coming with you."

She smiled a huge grin and hugged him tight, pressing her body against his. His heart began to speed up as he held her tight. Excitement flooded his veins with each quickening heartbeat. She didn't hold him long before she pulled away.

"Let's go then!" Her excitement matched his own. "Do you need to bring anything?"

He dashed inside to grab a change of clothes. Thankfully, Brad had left right before she'd arrived. Brad hadn't said he was leaving or where he was going but Kelsey knew he wouldn't be home for a few hours. He would find company either in a bottle at the bar or at the brothel. After their confrontation that afternoon, Kelsey didn't care what Brad was doing.

The rough purr of the Nissan's engine mingled with the blasting sound of air from the vents. It blew icy on his face, leaving his body feeling pleasantly warm. He didn't even know where they were going but already felt his body relax comfortably into the smooth fabric of the passenger seat. Jordyn was accelerating out of the driveway before he asked what her plan was. The small thrill of the unknown made him grin. It was a moment before she answered.

"I don't know, Kels," she said, looking sideways at him through her lashes and matching his relaxed grin. "Let's just drive and let the road take us away from here."

"Don't you have to work this weekend?"

"Nah, I got it off." She dismissed his concern with a shake of her head. "Who knows, maybe I'll never go back!"

Kelsey had been staring out the window, but looked sharply at her face as she said this. He studied her for a moment before she noticed. She caught his expression and laughed out loud.

"Don't be silly, Kels," she said. Her hands gripped the steering wheel, the white bones of her knuckles showing through her fair skin. "I couldn't ever leave my sister."

Not sharing in her assumed amusement, Kelsey watched her face as she spoke. Something was off. "Is your sister all that keeps you in this town?" Kelsey felt his voice lower, a deep tone in his chest that made her smile falter and her eyes flick to his, but only for a moment.

"And you, of course." Her tone was bright.

Kelsey made a low noncommittal noise. He didn't buy the answer, but didn't want to ruin the moment now. "Will she be alright with you gone?"

A frown creased her forehead at this. "Yea, I think so. We should only be gone for the weekend. I think Mama can handle that." Her tone implied that she wasn't confident in her mama's abilities. "Besides, I premade all their meals and asked Jeannie to check in on them at least once."

Kelsey leaned back in his seat, his knees pressed against the glove box. He turned his body so he could watch her as she drove. She smiled briefly again and flicked the radio on. Soft country twangs filled the car. He watched Jordyn's brown hair blowing softly back from her face. Her lips began to move to the words of the music.

So, she had been preparing for this trip long enough to make meals and make arrangements for someone to check in on Lizzie and her mom. He, meanwhile, hadn't any indication that she was planning this. He hadn't even known she was going to come over this evening until she'd called an hour before. Not that he was upset about it. He was thrilled. Their conversation a week ago had weighed heavy on their time together. Ever since they had decided to give it a chance, he had felt hope weave itself into the fabric of his life, much as he tried to prevent it. Just now, when she had said she would never go back home, even if it had been in jest, he couldn't help but feel those small strands of hope grow stronger and brighter.

She was singing along softly to the radio. Her voice was as sweet as honey in his ears. Her pointer finger tapped lightly on the steering wheel. The sun sank lower in the sky. Her skin glowed, gold and light with an undercurrent of faint pink flush. Her throat moved with the tones of the song and, instantly, he wanted to kiss her neck, to feel the smooth skin under his lips. He settled for leaning forward and kissing her shoulder, not wanting to startle her or stop her from singing. Without looking at him, she smiled through the song.

Though she was doing a fine job at seeming happy, Kelsey studied her harder to see if he could articulate what seemed off. An energy flowed from her, unlike anything he'd felt from her before. Her hands gripped the steering wheel too tightly. Her left foot tapped sporadically, ignoring the beat of the music. She glanced in the rearview mirror too frequently. Kelsey looked back, but the road stretched straight, flat and empty behind them.

Was she nervous then? About him? Surely they had been together now for enough time to prove that he wasn't going to take advantage of her. They had been alone together, even overnight. They'd had more than enough opportunity to sleep together. He thought he'd made it clear that he wanted better for her, much as he wanted to sleep with her.

And god, do I want to, he thought.

"You've got a look in your eyes." Her voice startled him from his musings. He attempted to smile but she laughed at him. "Oh, Kels. I do love you."

So much for making her feel safe around him. The look on his face must have revealed his thoughts because he watched her blush deepen and travel down her neck. He'd seen that before. He looked out the window so she couldn't see the desire in his eyes.

Get it together, Kelsey, he thought.

"So, really, where are we going?" Kelsey asked in an attempt to distract himself from the growing awareness of being on a weekend trip with her alone.

She fidgeted a bit in her seat before answering tentatively. "I was thinking Vegas."

Kelsey laughed. "Well, that's cliché."

She joined him in his laughter, though with an edge that made him uneasy.

"We live in the fucking middle of nowhere in Nevada, Kels. Where else do we go to get away from it all?"

"I'm not complaining. And I really don't care where we go. Take me to the moon." He settled himself into the space between the seat and car door. He let his head rest on the window, keeping one eye on Jordyn.

Her green eyes flashed at him. "What are you thinking about?"

"Just watchin' you..." he paused "...and wonderin' what flew into your bonnet today."

She smiled briefly, then bit her lip. "Kelsey, really, I'm fine." One hand left the steering wheel and she twined her fingers with his on her thigh. "I just think we need this. Let's be together and forget about home, okay?"

"I can do that." He squeezed her hand lightly and reached up to smooth away the tear that rolled warm and slow down the side of her cheek.

Chapter 13

THEIR EYES WERE GROWING heavy when the lights of the city started to twinkle ahead of them, but as the vibrant energy and lights of Las Vegas Boulevard grew steadily stronger, their sleepiness faded. Massive buildings, intricate architecture, glowing billboards and colorful people swirled around them as they drove, a cacophony of humanity. Kelsey had to remind himself they were going to stay for two nights so there was no need to put his neck out to take it all in now.

It was midnight when they made it down the strip to the Travelodge entrance. The small hotel was easy to miss due to the massive resorts threatening to swallow it up on both sides. A cerulean blue sign pointed down a short alley leading to a parking lot. The double story hotel surrounded the small lot; its matching blue doors opened to the outside.

A friendly Indian man confirmed the Travelodge's availability and checked them in. In an exhausted stupor, Kelsey and Jordyn left the lobby and stumbled to their first-floor room. After a few tries with the key, they entered and threw their things on the floor. Laughing giddily, they embraced and fell onto one of the squeaky queen beds.

The hotel room was dimly lit by two lamps with yellowing shades that sat on a matching set of faux mahogany veneered nightstands. A small black radio blinked the wrong time in neon red. The heavy green curtains were drawn tight against the city lights that glowed brightly outside the street level window. A boxy air conditioner blew icy air, whirring too loudly in the background. Kelsey and Jordyn lay exhausted, arms and legs sprawled dramatically on the bed.

Jordyn fell asleep almost immediately, unable to keep her eyes open, her head rested on Kelsey's arm. Kelsey couldn't sleep. Her body next to his, heavy in slumber, was stoking the fires of desire he'd tried so hard to keep extinguished over the last week. An ache in his groin, not unpleasant, caused him to shift his hips to find some relief from the tightness of his jeans. Jordyn stirred and he felt her hand move to the center of his chest. He shifted himself again. Her breathing remained the same and he wondered if she was still asleep.

The sound of her quiet voice let him know she wasn't. "Kelsey, I need to tell you something." Kelsey's stomach tightened. This was it. He was going to find out why she'd brought him here.

"Tonight?" he asked.

A short pause. "Yes. Tonight."

Kelsey brought a hand up to softly stroke her hair. "Go ahead," he murmured into the top of her head.

"I think I need to sit up for this."

Kelsey's stomach knotted further. He watched as she pushed herself up and noted that she wouldn't meet his eyes. She drew her knees into her chest and hugged them tightly. He scooted into a sitting position, nervously waiting. For a long minute, the only sound was blast of the air conditioner .

"It's about the day we met." Jordyn studied her hands. Kelsey studied the side of her face. "I was pregnant."

A deep crease formed between Kelsey's eyes. In a wild flurry of emotion, Kelsey madly wondered if it was his baby; but no, he hadn't even met her then. He hadn't even had sex with her now; of course it wasn't his. As this realization set in, his face fell and his shoulders slumped. He felt her watching him.

"I mean, up until that day I was pregnant. I lost the baby that day." Kelsey felt the crease return, but had no words. Mercifully, she continued so he didn't have to speak. "I was pretty far along, about 15 weeks. I went in to have an abortion." Her voice cracked as she went on. "But, I... I couldn't do it. I was on the table and I panicked. In that moment, lying there, ready for the baby to be taken from me, I suddenly thought of it as a human being instead of a curse. I ran out." Kelsey glanced up and saw that Jordyn's head now rested on her knees. A swell of emotion gave him strength to speak.

"Then how...?"

"That was a week before I met you," she interrupted him, her voice muffled into her knees. "The day I met you, nature took care of what I didn't." Suddenly her whole body was racked with sobs. Her hair fell around her knees and Kelsey saw tears roll down her thighs and soak into her shorts. He reached for her, unsure of what to do or say. He let his hand rest on her back, smoothing circles into the fabric of her shirt with his thumb. They sat for a long time, Jordyn crying and Kelsey at a loss.

When the tears no longer fell, Jordyn lifted her face to his. It was red and streaming, her eyes shining with raw pain. She spoke again, this time steadily meeting his eyes. "It hurt. A lot. I actually sort of went into labor when I had the miscarriage. I remember lying on the bathroom floor, writhing from the pain, hoping that Lizzie didn't find me there but wishing someone would come to take the pain away."

Jordyn searched his face, not for answers but for the strength to continue. He dropped his hand to grasp hers. She held it tightly; it hurt. "When the baby came out, I could...I could tell it was a boy..." Jordyn's eyes filled with fresh tears that rolled in a steady stream down her streaked cheeks. "It was so tiny." Her eyes became distant, seeing a room that wasn't in the hotel and a small bundle that fit in the palm of her hand.

Kelsey couldn't stand her anguish. He gathered her into his arms and pressed his cheek to the top of her head. She started to cry afresh. This time, Kelsey knew what to do. He just had to hold her. He just had to hold the pieces together because he needed her in one piece. He needed this woman.

Her weeping was like the tide, slowly rising and falling. Like the tide, it gradually receded. Her small hiccups tugged at his heart. He continued to hold her head close to his chest. His t-shirt was soaked with her tears, warm and damp against his skin. He forced his breaths to stay long and uniform until hers matched his own. A thought hit him.

"Did you think I wouldn't want you after that?" His question hung in the air.

Moments later he felt her nod against him.

"Oh, Darlin." His thumbs worked soft circles into the sides of her head as he searched for the right words. "After all we've done to each other, after all we've said, this makes me love you more."

"More?" The incredulity in her voice was apparent even though muffled by her stuffy nose and his chest.

"Yes, more," Kelsey replied, holding her closer, sensing the pieces were coming apart again. "The strength it took for you to get through that time is incredible. Don't get me wrong. I hate what you went through. I'm confused as shit about what to make of you being a prostitute and what that means for us. But you are a brave, mind-blowing woman. It took a lot of guts to tell me about it too. You could've kept it a secret." Kelsey didn't like the thought of secrets. He wanted all of her — wanted her body and soul.

"That's why I brought you here," Jordyn said softly.

"So you could tell me?"

"Yes. I thought it would be a neutral space and that...you could..."

"I could what?" Kelsey interrupted.

"Well, if you didn't want to see me anymore you could..."

"Leave you here?" Kelsey interrupted again.

"Well, yes," she replied meekly.

"Oh, Jordyn, you drive me crazy." Kelsey planted a kiss on the top of her head. "Even if I hated you, I could never leave you here."

Jordyn giggled nervously and hiccupped, causing her to snort into his shirt. A deep chuckle reverberated through his chest and she burrowed her face into him.

"So does this mean you are letting love be enough? Letting it fix us?" Jordyn sounded tentative.

Kelsey frowned. "If that's what I'm doing right now, then I guess...I am." Kelsey searched the silence of the room and found that he really meant it. Love was conquering all.

What a cliché, he thought.

"You realize what a shitty mess this all is?" Jordyn's voice held a smile. "I mean, really."

"Trust me, I know."

"But here we are..." Jordyn paused "...in Vegas."

They laughed together then, all their exhaustion, emotion and relief crushing them back onto the bed.

"Go to sleep now, Darlin.'" Kelsey pulled her in close.

She wiggled her legs, kicking off her shoes. He did the same. Without bothering to change clothes or get under the bed covers, she put her head in the now familiar spot on his arm and was asleep within a minute. Kelsey reached for the lamp and clicked it off.

He lay awake for another couple minutes staring into the darkness. Her soft weight against him felt like a miracle. Against all reason, there she was and he couldn't be happier. He felt a tear prickle in the corner of his eye. Fatigue washed over him, warm and irresistible. His eyes closed, and the tear rolled silently down his cheek.

Chapter 14

KELSEY AND JORDYN ROLLED out of bed, rumpled and groggy, at noon after their late night. After getting cleaned up, eating a burger at McDonald's and a donut at Krispy Kreme, they let time slip away as they explored the nearby Circus Circus hotel. Night fell fast over the desert and Las Vegas Boulevard. When darkness fell, they decided to walk the strip to see the lights.

"I'm going to stop in here for cigarettes." Kelsey motioned to a brightly lit store front.

A yellowing sign imprinted with dirty white letters — reading 'Mini-Mart' — hung along the edge of the single-story building tucked between two imposing hotels. A myriad of multi-colored t-shirts, socks, underwear and kitschy paraphernalia on a half-dozen racks littered the sidewalk in front of the store. A constant stream of pedestrians flowed by the front, with one or two breaking off occasionally to browse through the contents of the mini-mart. A short round man in a neon green t-shirt, reading 'girls-girls-girls', stood near the entrance. He flicked a stack of cards for the girls in question complete with naked photos and phone numbers. Kelsey passed by the man with barely a glance, having passed by dozens like him already.

"I'll hang out here," Jordyn said and motioned to a relatively uncrowded area next to the store.

"Are you sure?" Kelsey asked.

"I'm sure." She smiled reassuringly.

Kelsey gave her a quick kiss on the cheek and squeezed her hand. He dodged a young couple exiting the store and went inside.

It was easy to get distracted in the souvenir shop. Several times Kelsey had to remind himself that Jordyn waited alone outside. Finally wading through the array of odds and ends, he made it to the counter. He bought the cigarettes along with a blinking 'Welcome to Las Vegas' keychain for Jordyn. Shoving the box of cigarettes into his front pocket and the keychain into his jeans pocket, he walked out of the store.

He didn't immediately spot Jordyn. While scanning the throng of people outside, he pulled a cigarette and lighter out of his pocket. He lit up and inhaled deeply. Thinking she must have decided to go inside the store, he turned and looked inside. Not seeing her there, he walked to the side of the store near the alley where she said she would wait. Before he turned into the alley, he heard her voice. He stopped to listen.

"How long you been doing this?" Jordyn was saying, her tone conversational.

A bolder woman's voice answered her. "A year."

"Is that your pimp?" Jordyn asked.

Kelsey took a convulsive step forward and glanced around the side of the building. Ten feet from him, Jordyn leaned against the painted concrete side of the mini-mart next to another woman. A dark sedan with black tinted windows sat fifty yards down the alley with its lights on. No one else was around. The women didn't seem to be in danger and Jordyn was engrossed in their conversation. Since they hadn't seen him, Kelsey took a small step back to listen.

"Yea, that's him. I'm waiting on a customer," the woman answered.

Kelsey chanced another look around the corner. The woman was wearing a leather black coat. A bright blue dress peeked out from below the coat, tightly hugging her butt and upper thighs. She wore impossibly high silver heels. Long platinum hair hid her face from him. He could see she held an unlit cigarette in her hand. The woman reminded him of a uneasy bird, her body tense, her head constantly swiveling at every noise.

"Is business good here?" Jordyn asked. Kelsey's heart fell into his stomach. Why was she asking that?

"Real good," the woman replied. "My new pimp's got me a really good rate." Jordyn's body was angled away so he couldn't see her face, but he watched her head nod slowly up and down.

The woman raised the cigarette to her mouth and flicked a lighter on with her other hand. He could see her hands shaking from where he stood. Jordyn saw too.

"Here let me help." He heard Jordyn softly say. She cupped the woman's shaky hand in hers, steadying it. Jordyn helped bring the lighter next to the cigarette tip. It glowed orange as the woman inhaled. He saw a brief ruby red smile peek from around the woman's hair.

"It's these fucking crazy drugs the doc's got me on," the woman said. "Can't even light a damn cigarette without shaking."

"I'm sorry," Jordyn said, voice still soft.

Kelsey saw the woman take a long look at Jordyn. "What about you? You have a pretty face, nice ass, great tits. You want a job?"

Jordyn laughed lightly. "I just got out of it. But thanks for the offer."

"No shit," the woman said and took another long inhale on her cigarette.

"Yea. I was in it for three years. Good money."

"Why did you quit? You get beat?"

"No, my customers and madam were all good to me. I enjoyed it at first. It just started to fuck me up, you know?"

Kelsey watched the woman nod. She reached into her jacket and withdrew a cigarette and offered it to Jordyn. Jordyn took it, as well as the lighter the woman presented. Moments later a cloud of smoke rose up around Jordyn's shadowed face.

Jordyn sighed. "I just saw too much shit happen. Well...you know," she said.

The woman nodded.

"One of my customers left me a Bible once," Jordyn said, causing the woman to laugh. "I know, right?" Jordyn continued, briefly joining in the woman's laughter.

"Did you throw it at him?" the woman asked dryly.

"Almost," Jordyn replied. "But I didn't. And then I read it."

The woman turned her face so Kelsey could see it more clearly. She was eyeing Jordyn skeptically with dark-lined eyes. "You aren't from the god-damn church are you?" The woman stood up and away from the wall as she spoke, ready to move.

"Nah, I've never been to a church before." Kelsey could hear the smile in Jordyn's voice.

The woman relaxed against the wall. "Cheers to that," she said, raising her cigarette in salute. "Those bitches don't know anything about me or the street." She leaned her head back and closed her eyes.

"But I did read that Bible," Jordyn continued. "Mostly the parts about Jesus. I liked how gentle he was."

"I love a gentle man," the woman said slowly, blowing smoke into the warm night air.

"Did you know the Bible tells stories about Jesus and hookers?" Jordyn asked the woman. Kelsey heard her voice quicken.

"No shit? Jesus was a John. Who knew."

"No, not a John," Jordyn replied. "He basically treated them like anybody else. He taught them stuff. Gave them the time of day."

The woman grunted and let Jordyn continue.

"I was impressed so I started to read everything else Jesus said. He offered hope and love in a shit world. Hope and love that is totally independent of what I do. And that is something a hooker can appreciate." Jordyn laughed dryly.

The woman raised her hand in acknowledgement again.

"Anyway, I was offered a way out, took it, and I haven't looked back."

"Glad you found happiness, Hon. But I've found my happiness out here. At least the happiness I deserve. That Bible shit isn't for everyone." The woman flicked her cigarette into the alley and ground it into the pavement with one spiked heel.

"Thanks for the smoke," Jordyn said.

Ruby red lips smiled briefly. A short honk sounded from the dark sedan down the alley followed by two flashes of the headlights. The woman gave Jordyn a lopsided grin and nodded once. Without another word she turned and walked toward the sedan, long body framed by the headlights.

Jordyn turned toward Kelsey and spotted him right away. She met his eyes, took a long inhale on her cigarette and threw it onto the ground in front of her. She used her sneaker to put it out.

When she joined him at his side, he wrapped an arm around her shoulders. "I thought you didn't smoke anymore," he said into her ear conspiratorially. She glanced sheepishly up at him and shrugged her shoulders as they started down the Boulevard again.

"I wanted an excuse to talk to her," she said quietly.

Kelsey paused. "I think I knew that."

Jordyn threaded her arm smoothly around his middle and squeezed.

...

They walked in silence, each occupied with their own thoughts. Kelsey didn't know what to say about the woman in the alley, and Jordyn didn't seem to want to talk about it.

The mini-mart wasn't far from the Travelodge and Jordyn asked to change her shoes before they walked farther. The door to their room clicked closed behind them. Jordyn plopped down on the edge of the bed and took off a sneaker.

She sighed and rubbed her foot. "I thought these would be good to wear, but I need more support I guess. It's a lot farther to walk than I thought!"

"Let me know if you need me to carry you," Kelsey said, a smile in his voice. He raised his right arm and flexed his bicep.

"Thanks, I will," Jordyn said, rolling her eyes.

Kelsey sat down on the second bed and watched her change into a worn pair of running shoes, mentally noting that a new pair would be a good gift idea someday. His gaze traveled to her backpack, contents spilling from the open top. A corner of the leather Bible peaked out from the dark insides.

Kelsey's stomach tightened as he remembered Jordyn's conversation with the woman.

"I wondered about that Bible," he said, not looking away from it.

She glanced at the Bible, then quickly to his face. Her eyes lingered on him, gauging his mood. He met her gaze and she looked away.

"Oh yea." Jordyn finished tying her shoe and let her foot fall softly to the carpeted floor. "Were you listening to us the whole time?"

"I think most of it."

Jordyn folded her hands in her lap and turned her body toward him. She looked back into his eyes with a piercing green stare before she spoke. "He was a preacher, a regular who I'd never seen before. The other girls liked him because he...well, he was a nice guy." Jordyn glanced nervously down at her lap and back to his face. "Do you really want me to tell you about this? I know it's hard." A frown creased the space between her eyes. He resisted the impulse to smooth it.

"I want to know." Kelsey was surprised to hear his voice sound steady. He felt like he was being strangled.

She searched his face again, checking for sincerity. Satisfied with what she saw, she continued, "Afterward, I thought he was asleep. So, I got up to grab a glass of water from the table by the door. His bag was open. I saw that book inside." She reached over and grabbed the Bible from her bag. She set it carefully, almost reverently, on the top of her thighs and spread her fingers wide over the cover.

"I didn't know it was a Bible but I thought it might be fun to do some reading. I never could sleep with the customers."

She shook her head as if to rid herself of the memory and took a deep wavering breath. "I opened it to the place where he had the ribbon place holder. I figured out really quickly that it was a Bible and almost closed it. I stopped though, because some of the words on the page were written in red. I wondered why. I started reading the red words. A lot of them were confusing to me. I figured out that the red words were when Jesus spoke. The part I was reading intrigued me. Jesus was talking to His Father." Jordyn looked shyly at him, hand still resting on the cover of the Bible. "I, ah...memorized it if you want to hear."

Kelsey was horrified and fascinated. He hadn't seen her talk this way before. She was calm and sure, peaceful and pleading. She wanted him to hear, but he didn't know if he wanted to. He loved her and wanted more than life to know her, but this might be too much. He closed his eyes.

"Go ahead." This time his voice was tight.

He heard a soft intake of breath before she began.

"'I praise you, Father, Lord of heaven and earth, because you have hidden these things from the wise and learned, and revealed them to little children. Yes, Father, for this is what you were pleased to do.

"'All things have been committed to me by my Father. No one knows the Son except the Father, and no one knows the Father except the Son and those to whom the Son chooses to reveal him.

"'Come to me, all you who are weary and burdened, and I will give you rest. Take my yoke upon you and learn from me, for I am gentle and humble in heart, and you will find rest for your souls. For my yoke is easy and my burden is light.'"

Jordyn let the last words hang in the air. Kelsey opened his eyes to find hers closed, but relaxed. When she opened them, they were gleaming with tears. She focused on him and leaned forward, voice light and quick with passion.

"I could only think of Lizzie at first. Except for what little I can provide, Lizzie has never had anything given to her, nothing good happen to her, and no one to truly care about her. But she is always hopeful, always sweet, despite all the shit that is handed to her. Those little red words that I read told me that God gave Himself to Lizzie before the smartasses and rich people. That Lizzie had something they didn't. And the words told me that it made God happy to do it. I couldn't believe it!" A real tear rolled down Jordyn's cheek, though she wasn't crying. Kelsey sat silently, tongue thick and dry in his mouth.

"If Lizzie knew God, it made sense: her joy, her hope, her love. It all made sense. But then those last words hit me hard. At the time, I could've sworn that someone pushed me here." She pressed one finger into the center of her breast bone. "But no one did, I checked." The corner of her mouth turned up into a crooked smile.

"Those words spoke to me, Kels." She continued to push softly into her chest, emphasizing her words. "'Come to me, all you who are weary and burdened...' That was me: tired beyond words and tormented by doubt and worry. He said, 'Learn from me, for I am gentle and humble in heart, and you will find rest for your souls...' Just the words felt like a perfectly cool drink of water after working outside on a long hot day. I could almost imagine it flowing through my throat and chest and into my gut. Nothing like the drink of real water I'd taken just a few minutes before." Kelsey swallowed, feeling his own mouth, still dry. He licked his lower lip, trying to soothe the parched sensation.

"Jesus said 'My burden is light...' And that was it. I was hooked." Jordyn let her hand fall back into her lap. "I was suddenly blindsided with the knowledge that not only did God know that I was weary and burdened, but he offered me rest. He offered me a way out from the shit I had done and was continuing to do. Not only a way out, but he offered me love. I couldn't be the same after that. I had hope then, and real love stared at me from the pages of that Bible. I had to find out more."

Kelsey moved his mouth to speak but no sound came. He cleared his throat and tried again. "Back when you were talking to the hooker in the alley, you said the man, your client, gave you the Bible?"

"He did. I thought he was sleeping, and maybe he was at first, but as I was reading, he spoke to me. I remember he laughed when he startled me. He asked what I was reading, but changed his mind before I told him. He said he didn't want to think about work right then. He got up and dressed. Then before he left, he tossed the Bible on the bed." Jordyn paused. When she continued her voice was broken with tears. "He told me that a whore needed it more than he did." Her head fell into her hands and her back shook with sobs.

Kelsey couldn't keep himself from holding her. Anger at the man swelled within him. He felt like punching through the door. Instead, he crossed the space between them, sat down on the bed next to her and pulled her shaking body close.

"Fuck him," Kelsey said into her hair. Attempting to channel his rage, he continued, "Forget about him. How can you find hope and love in a book that guy had had his fucking hands on? I'd like to get my fucking hands on him." Kelsey could feel the heat surging through his face, down his arms and thighs.

Jordyn raised her head from her hands and turned to look at him. Her eyes shone from the tears that rolled steadily down her pale pink cheeks. She put both hands on the sides of his face and kissed him softly.

"Oh, Kels," she said, voice tender and insistent. "Don't you see? That man was one of the wise and learned who Jesus talked about. God gave Himself to Lizzie, and He gave Himself to me, but that man didn't know what he had. He didn't know God." She glanced down, shaking her head, eyes moving back and forth, searching his chest for answers to unasked questions.

"So what, Jordyn? You just forgive the dick-head and move on?" Kelsey's voice was still unstable, unwilling to let the man's words go.

Shining green eyes met his again. "I have to."

Kelsey stood up abruptly. "Jesus Christ, Jordyn." He waved one hand in the air in annoyance and paced a few steps. "Sorry. It's just..." As abruptly as he had stood up, he kneeled in front of her, grasping her hands in his. His heart beat pounded hard in his ears as he pressed his forehead to their clasped hands. He began again, stifling the emotion that threatened to burst from him. "It's just that I love you." Another swell rose into his throat. He swallowed to push it down. "I love you and I can't see you hurt." He rested his head on their hands.

"I know, Kels." He felt her cheek press against the back of his head.

His knees throbbed and his back ached before his thoughts were coherent. His breathing slowed to match hers. She lifted her head and squeezed his hands as he shifted his stiff body. Her fingers wove into his roughened hair and her palm cupped his ear, moving his face to meet hers.

"You don't have to understand," she said softly against his lips. "But I just need you to be okay with it. With me. With who I was and who I am."

Kelsey let out a heavy breath. "Jordyn." He searched her face. "I don't understand. I hear your hope and happiness. I can see your conviction over the red words in the Bible. But I can't forgive that pastor bastard. I can't forgive anyone who has hurt you." Kelsey shook his head and placed his hands on her face. Her cheeks were warm and soft. He held them lightly, keeping her eyes on his. "But I am okay with who you were and who you are. I'm more than okay. I know that your past has made you who you are, and as much as that hurts to think about, I wouldn't change you, Darlin.'" He smoothed his thumb over her cheek bone. "Do you hear me? I wouldn't change a damn thing."

Tears pooled and spilled from her shining green eyes, skipping down her cheeks and over his thumb, landing silently on the leather-covered Bible below them. Mouth open in wordless response, she nodded. He closed the inches between them to press his mouth to hers. Dropping his hands, he twisted his arms around her waist and pulled her closer. Their kisses deepened and the world melted away. His breathing quickened with hers, their chests rising and falling like the waves of a stormy ocean.

He couldn't get close enough. His body ached to take her, knowing that it was the only way to feel close enough. His hand slid up her thigh. He reveled in the feel of her heated body through the rough jean material under his fingers. Her own fingers tangled in the hair at the back of his neck. Her mouth pressed hard to his, moving in breathtaking synchronization. He slid his hand up farther, just touching the crease between her thighs.

He stopped.

The Bible.

Damn it, he thought and grabbed the Bible that his fingers had reached. His muscles tensed to throw it on the floor, but he stopped again. She felt him pause, and pulled away slightly. She looked down to her lap, where he clutched the worn book tightly in his hand. Her fingers hovered over his hand and finally rested on it.

"Kels, you don't—" she began.

"Yes, I do." His voice was tight as a tripwire. "I do have to stop." His knuckles whitened and he turned dark, tortured eyes to her. "Don't you see? I have to stop."

Jordyn shook her head and made a confused noise in protest.

"Just stop. Sit. Let me think for a second." Kelsey stood up, Bible still in hand. He paced for a minute, then turned to face her.

"I don't want to sleep with another whore," Kelsey finally said.

Jordyn's mouth fell open, her brow creased and shoulders slumped. Kelsey immediately knew his mistake and quickly knelt in front of her again. "Oh god, no." He cupped her face.

"No, no, no. That's not what—" A warm tear fell onto his arm. "Shit. I really fucked this one up."

He took an unsteady breath. "I just... I want something different. For both of us." Another wavering inhale. "I don't want to be that pastor or any other man who's taken you like some kind of thing to be used and discarded. I've done that to women. And it's bullshit." More hot tears splashed on his arms from her downturned face. "And I don't want you to feel used again. I've seen the woman inside your beautiful body and that woman deserves way more than to be used like a tool." As the tears steadily dripped onto his arms, he smoothed the shiny brown hair around her ear.

"I have to stop," he whispered.

When the tears stopped falling, she pulled her head up and looked into his face with streaming red eyes. She sniffed and a small nervous laugh bubbled from her shaking chest. "Kelsey Campbell, I do love you."

"Thank god," Kelsey said, turning his eyes upward and pulling her into a tight embrace. He felt her body shake from either laughter or sobs; he couldn't tell. It didn't matter though, because she was holding him tighter than he was holding her.

Chapter 15

THEIR WORLD WAS AWASH with the glowing colors of the rainbow. All the elements were present — fire, water and gritty earth below their feet. Neon lights bathed the faces of thousands of people moving together in a seething mass of civilization. Every corner of the earth seemed to be represented in the people; different languages and accents, different ages and genders; booze, drugs, money and sex oozed from their pores. Shocking energy and seductive carnality surged in an inexorable current down the Boulevard.

Kelsey and Jordyn followed the flow, marveling at their surroundings and people. They walked for nearly an hour to the magnificent fountains at the Bellagio, crossed the Boulevard and stood for a while under the Eiffel tower at the Paris Hotel and Casino. Neither spoke much but they occasionally exchanged knowing smiles and shocked expressions as they walked hand in hand, squeezing tight to one another. They turned down dozens of propositions for tickets to elaborate shows, coupons for cheap food and flyers giving the opportunity to enjoy countless flavors of sexual diversions. Even if they had the money, they didn't have the desire. For now, their hands twined together was enough.

Between the Paris Hotel and Casino and another sprawling shopping complex a small crowd was gathered. The crowd was fluid, ebbing and flowing around its core. People of every shape and size stopped, giggling and shouting lewd encouragement to the center of the huddle. With an understanding nod of mild interest, Kelsey and Jordyn ambled closer. When they were near enough to see clearly, they stopped and Kelsey pulled Jordyn close to his side.

Two women wearing flamboyant feathered headdresses and little else stood beckoning passersby to have their picture taken alongside them. Each boasted huge tanned breasts, their nipples covered by sequined stickers with matching tassels. A string thong overlaid in similarly colored sequins showed off their perky behinds and barely covered their waxed groins. Each wore eight inch heels on four inch platform shoes, maneuvering them with confident poise. The women's faces were elaborate as well. Thickly applied makeup in garish colors effectively hid every inch of natural skin.

Kelsey glanced down at Jordyn, who didn't seem phased by the outlandish spectacle in front of them. Her expression was one of contented interest. Her long eyelashes blinked slowly as she watched. Kelsey felt his mouth transform into a relaxed smile. He thought he knew what she was feeling because he felt it too: untempted, unphased and immune to the sensual pull that everyone around them felt. He felt both peacefully observant of the world around him and wholly captivated by the woman at his side. He felt and heard her every breath despite the raucous crowd around them. He watched her face, the way her mouth moved, the way her nose wrinkled and her ears moved up when she smiled. He smelled the sweet floral-honey essence of her through the throng of humanity.

The two women in front of them winked at Kelsey and beckoned him forward. One woman, wearing predominately red, puckered her lips and blew a kiss. The other woman, wearing baby blue, shook her breasts at him with an enticing smile. A few inebriated observers shouted encouragements. Kelsey waved them off with a firm hand. Sensing his disinterest, the women quickly turned their attention to one of the men who had shouted at Kelsey.

A pudgy red-faced man in khaki shorts and a Hawaiian shirt waddled up to them, a dull grin on his unfocused face. His companions hollered reinforcement at him, holding their disposable cameras at the ready. The pudgy man wedged himself between the two woman and playfully flicked the nipple tassels of the woman in red. She laughed brightly and posed for the camera. Picture taken, the pudgy man fumbled in his pocket for a crumpled five-dollar bill and handed it to the women. They both smiled at him, perfectly white teeth behind bright red lips. Before the pudgy man reached his companions, another man was already standing with the women, playing with their tassels and trying to grab their breasts.

Jordyn leaned her head against his chest. Her movement and the trust that guided it caused his heart to beat twice in quick succession. A tightness in his throat made him swallow. He leaned his lips into her hair and kissed her slowly. Peering down her nose, he could see her mouth move into a smile. His heart beat twice again. He paused with his lips hovering over the part in her hair, his own breath radiating hot against his skin.

"Marry me."

His words were a whisper, a breath into the riotous night air.

The top of her head moved up and against his lips, an acknowledgment.

"Marry me."

Again, a whisper.

And again, an acknowledgement. She turned her head, her bright green eyes full of question.

Kelsey gently gripped her shoulders and turned her willingly toward him, their faces inches apart. Her breath was warm on his face. He felt it tingle against his lips. His forehead dropped softly against hers, held with a magnetic force.

"Darlin', I love you. Marry me."

Her eyes searched his own, asking if he meant what he said. It took only a moment to find the answer. He did mean it, body and soul.

Kelsey watched her chest rise and fall. Her lips parted. Instead of speaking she nodded against him. His heart skipped a beat, restarting double time.

"Was that a yes?" he said breathlessly.

She nodded again and said, "Yes." At once, her eyes shone with tears and a smile lit her face. "It was a yes, yes, yes." She reached for his waist.

Kelsey felt his own smile match hers, watt for watt. He pulled her body close, foreheads still together. He couldn't find any words.

A bold voice cut through his fog of happiness. "Well? Aren't you going to kiss her?" The voice came from the woman in red. She was smirking at them from her place next to the newest patron.

Kelsey didn't need to be prompted again. With one hand on Jordyn's lower back, the other on the base of her neck, he pulled her close and covered her lips with his own. The two women, the gathered crowd, the grand casinos and the neon lights slipped away. They flowed like mercury into the earth, leaving the two of them alone, bound together in love.

Chapter 16

"WHAT ARE YOU WEARING?" Jordyn asked as she reached up to tug lightly on the edge of his new black vest. Despite the effort to tease him, her whole face lit up with a brilliantly beautiful smile. Her bright green eyes were lit from within, a burning furnace, warm and light and all for him.

"What?" he replied with mock indignation. "This old thing?" He pulled at the front of the vest he'd found at a nearby Target store. He was feigning nervousness but found he actually felt it. He looked into her angel's face, shining with emotion.

"That old thing?" she said as her hands reached out to reverently touch the button on his shirt. He stood up straighter as she examined him, softly stroking the fabric of his shirt and vest. She took a step back to look at his jeans and tennis shoes, the same he'd worn the last two days. She giggled. He shuffled his feet self-consciously. "There you are, Kels," she whispered to herself. She looked up from his shoes and smiled wider than before.

"I couldn't find any new shoes and the jeans just looked okay, I guess. I didn't think..." Kelsey trailed off as she put her palm over his mouth.

"I love it. I love them." Her blue eyes shone with tears again and her hand fell away. She leaned her head against his chest. He tipped her chin up and kissed her mouth lightly. Jordyn suddenly shoved him and backed away.

"Hey! Don't you know it's bad luck to kiss the bride before the ceremony?" She scrubbed her lips with the back of her hand.

"Uh, nope. I never heard that." The corner of Kelsey's mouth quirked into a smile.

"Hm. Well, it is. I'm pretty sure anyway…" She frowned, then returned his smile.

"Hold on, hold on, Darlin'. Look at you!" Kelsey took a step back and held her arms to look at her appraisingly. He'd been too nervous about his clothes and captivated by her smile to notice what she was wearing.

She looked down at her dress, hands smoothing it over her abdomen, and looked anxiously back to his face. The corner of her mouth curved unwittingly upward.

"You like it?"

In response, he grasped her shoulders and pulled her in for another kiss, deeper this time. She melted into him for a moment. Suddenly remembering herself, she pushed him away.

"What did we just talk about?" She laughed at him and wiped her lips again.

Kelsey ignored her comment. "Let me get a better look."

She obediently stood still while he looked at her. She wore a simple white summer dress, somewhat form-fitting and long enough to reach her mid-thigh. Her long hair cascaded in loose curls over her bare shoulders and chest, the soft curve of her breasts was just visible above the line of her dress. Her smooth legs stretched long to her feet, which were clad in white flip-flops, toes painted coral. He looked back to her face, which was flushed pink from his appraisal and rubbing the kisses from her lips. He vaguely noticed that she hadn't put any makeup on, but he didn't care. She was a bridal angel.

"You look perfect." He held out his hand and she took it, smiling shyly from behind the curtain of brown hair that fell loose around her face. "I can't wait to get a peek under the hood," he said, waggling his eyebrows.

She shoved him again, halfheartedly this time. He chastely kissed the top of her head and pulled her close. He felt her take a deep breath, hold it for a moment and let it out, hot on his chest.

"Are you ready?" he whispered into her hair.

She nodded. "I am."

The Chapel of Rock n' Roll was within walking distance of the Travelodge. Hand in hand they entered and were greeted by a blond woman. She was alternating between smoking a cigarette and tapping away on a desktop computer keyboard. She glanced at them, continuing to type. Sharing an unsure expression, they approached.

"We saw a sign outside that said $99 to get married?" Kelsey asked the side of the woman's head. She looked up at them, her absurdly long, fake eyelashes blinking slowly.

"Starts at $99," she said pointedly, raising one pencil thin eyebrow. "Look at this." She grabbed a colorful laminated paper from beside her and tossed it lightly onto the desk.

"Thanks," Kelsey said, his response sounding more like a question.

As they began to read through the wedding packages offered, Jordyn snorted softly. In addition to the traditional ceremony, both indoor and outdoor, the Chapel of Rock n' Roll offered ceremonies conducted by Elvis or Little Elvis. They exchanged surprised glances as Jordyn mouthed the words 'Little Elvis'. Kelsey smiled lopsidedly. He tossed the laminated sheet onto the desk.

"I think we'd like a traditional ceremony," he said.

"We can't do that," the woman replied, turning in her swiveling chair and placing her hands together in front of her. Her lime green fingernails tapped on the desk as if she were still typing.

"Okay…" Kelsey said, puzzled.

"I mean, we can't do that today. All booked." She raised a thin dark eyebrow at him.

"Okay," Kelsey said and looked at Jordyn. The phone next to the computer rang shrilly and the woman swiveled back to answer it.

"I guess we just go then?" Kelsey asked Jordyn, who looked crestfallen. She nodded. Kelsey turned to thank the woman at the desk, but thought better of it.

As they reached the door, the woman called to them. "Good news. Cancellation. But you'll have to head back right now if you want to get this done."

Jordyn's mouth dropped open and Kelsey smiled widely. "Sounds good," he said.

"Do you guys need a witness?"

"Yes."

"Alright, come with me." The woman pushed herself up, teetering on high heels that matched her fingernails. She tugged the hem of her mini skirt down and headed through a crimson door in the back wall. She beckoned them over her shoulder with a backward wave. Not pausing to check Jordyn's reaction, Kelsey grabbed her hand and pulled her along.

It turned out that the woman in lime was the witness, and that an Elvis impersonator, full size, would be administering their ceremony — no extra charge. The lime woman plopped into a single folding chair that sat atop a red carpet in front of what she called the 'stage'. The Elvis impersonator stood in the center of the stage, floppy black wig slightly askew. He grabbed his black lapels with both thumbs and adjusted the gold-sequined suit jacket, swaying his hips smoothly back and forth. Jordyn laughed nervously as she watched Elvis and noticed the backdrop for the chapel. A canvas covered the wall behind Elvis. It was printed with a picture of an actual stage complete with lights, a drum set and a vintage Shure microphone. A haze of cigarettes and dust lightly clouded the air. 1970's rock music blared as they approached the 'stage'. When they arrived on stage, they stood, framing Elvis. The woman in lime pushed herself up from the squeaking metal chair and reached for a small knob on the wall. She turned it and the music lowered to a tolerable decibel level.

"Are you ready to get married?" Elvis projected loudly into the room as he flashed double 'rock-on' signs with his hands.

Jordyn laughed shortly and Kelsey grinned. They both nodded, trying to keep from dissolving into hilarity. They reached for each other's hands and squeezed tightly.

The vows were brief and basic but delivered with all the pomp expected from a Las Vegas wedding administered by the King himself. Despite the theatrics, the contrived Elvis impersonation and the disinterested woman in lime, everything evaporated around Jordyn and Kelsey as they said their vows.

"Let's exchange the rings, baby!" Elvis's voice broke through their trance. They looked open-mouthed into his face, a smile plastered around chalk white teeth.

The haze of happiness fell away from Kelsey's eyes at the same time Jordyn's eyes widened.

They didn't have rings.

Kelsey stared at Elvis, then glanced back at the woman in lime who raised her thin eyebrow, and turned back to Elvis. "We don't..." He paused. "Hold on!" Kelsey dropped one of Jordyn's hands and plunged his hand into his jeans pocket. He retrieved the blinking Las Vegas keychain he'd purchased for Jordyn the night before. It had a round circle of metal on it and it was going to have to work. He smiled sheepishly at her. Jordyn raised her eyebrows and smiled delightedly.

"That will work!" Elvis said.

Kelsey gave Jordyn the ring. She held out her upturned left hand. He slid the circle onto her ring finger and placed the plastic piece, blinking brightly, into her palm. She closed her fingers around it, looked up at him and stood on tiptoes to kiss him. He kissed her back, surprised.

"Now hold on there! Keep your panties on, Little Lady. I haven't said to kiss the bride yet." Elvis chuckled.

It was Jordyn's turn to smile sheepishly now. When it was her turn to give Kelsey a ring, she took the keychain off her finger and put it on Kelsey's. He leaned forward to kiss her solidly on the mouth and backed away with a piercing look at Elvis that dared him to say something. Elvis chuckled again.

"Not that you two need me to say anything...but you may now kiss the bride!" Elvis concluded the ceremony. On cue the woman in lime flicked the volume on the music back up. Kelsey and Jordyn embraced, kissing deeply, only pulling away when laughter consumed them both.

...

They stepped out of the Chapel of Rock n' Roll. The heat boiling off the strip snatched their breath and blew their hair. Jordyn grabbed Kelsey's hand and they turned to each other, forgetting the heat to press their bodies together. Sweat instantly formed on their skin. Another couple pushed past them to get inside the chapel. They shuffled to the side, not breaking their hold.

Jordyn eventually leaned back from his face, still clinging to his waist. She craned her neck to look behind her, searching for his hands. "Can I see it?"

Kelsey produced a copy of their marriage certificate, issued by the State of Nevada. Jordyn took it from his hand and read through it slowly. Finally finishing, she looked up at him with an open-mouthed grin. "You know the woman who witnessed our ceremony? Her name is Crystal Destiny — do you think that's her real name?"

"If it isn't her real name, let's hope the State of Nevada doesn't care."

"Elvis's real name is Dick Swett." Jordyn paused and Kelsey laughed convulsively. It took her a moment to realize why he was laughing.

"No wonder he wants to impersonate someone else for a living," Jordyn said between bubbles of laughter as she wiped her eyes of gleeful tears.

"We won't soon forget this, Darlin'," Kelsey said, wrapping his arms around her again.

"For more reason than just the names of our officiator," Jordyn said, snuggling closer and squeezing him tight. "Is that your phone buzzing, or are you really ready to get back to our hotel?" She winked up at him.

"Oh, my phone. I mean, I'm ready to get back to the hotel too...but..." He used his free hand to retrieve the vibrating phone from his pocket. He blinked away the glare of the sun to see the tiny screen. "It's my sister."

"Go ahead." Jordyn smiled encouragingly and rested her head against his chest.

Kelsey flipped the phone open. "Hey, Sis."

Anne's vibrant voice made him smile. "Hi, Kels! Catch you at a bad time?"

"Ah, no. What's up?"

"Well..." She paused dramatically. "I'm going to come see you tomorrow! Surprise!"

"Oh, okay," he said, stunned, his fingers moved in mindless circles on Jordyn's back.

"Maybe you could fake being happy?" Anne's voice remained bright. "I am your only sister, you know!"

"Yea, definitely. It's just that I was maybe planning on being gone tomorrow."

"That's fine. I'll just hang with old Pops and you'll come rescue me when you can."

"Anne... I don't want you to be there with him alone. He's not..." As he spoke, Jordyn bent her head back to look into his face and gripped his arm.

Anne interrupted. "Kels, I think I can handle Brad. I'll take off and visit some old friends if I need to."

"We'll make it work. We can be home tomorrow," Jordyn whispered to Kelsey. He frowned. "It's alright. Really. We have forever."

Kelsey searched her eyes before replying. "Anne, I'll change my plans. I'll see you tomorrow."

"Ah shucks. All for me? Perfect. I can't wait."

"Me either. I have a surprise for you too."

"What did you do? Run off to Vegas and marry that girl?" Anne laughed hysterically at herself. Kelsey was stunned again. When he didn't answer right away, Anne's laughter abruptly stopped. "Wait, Kels, did you really do that?"

He recovered quickly. "I said it was a surprise."

"Damn, Kelsey!"

"Goodbye, Annie," Kelsey said pointedly, attempting to silence her.

"You are one crazy motherfucker." Kelsey flicked his phone shut and cut off Anne's voice. Kelsey's grin stretched from cheekbone to cheekbone.

"Are you sure that it's okay to go home tomorrow?" Kelsey asked Jordyn sincerely, thrilled with the idea that he was going to be able to introduce his sister to his new wife.

"Yes, Kels. I'm sure." She squeezed his biceps reassuringly. "I'm really excited to meet your sister. You guys obviously love each other very much."

"We do." Kelsey kissed her firmly. Then he squinted conspiratorially at her. "I guess we will have to fit a whole honeymoon into one night."

She pressed her lips together in a smirk and pushed her torso against his. "We'd better get started then."

Kelsey didn't need any more encouragement.

Chapter 17

WHEN THEY ARRIVED BACK at the Travelodge, the front desk clerk spotted them and ran out. Kelsey and Jordyn exchanged confused expressions as Kelsey greeted the anxious-looking clerk.

"I'm sorry to say you failed to check out at the appropriate time and we had to remove your belongings from the room. They are in the lobby. You can pay your balance when you gather your things." He paused. "And there is no vacancy at this time. A large convention is in town." The clerk bowed his head apologetically and backed across the parking lot and into the swinging door of the lobby.

Kelsey sighed heavily through his lips. A deep frown furrowed his brow as he looked at his new bride, now devoid of a place to spend her wedding night. She was watching him with an amused turn of her mouth. He shrugged and she grinned.

"Let's go camping," she said and started toward the door of the lobby.

Shaking his head, he marched after her to grab their bags.

An hour later, the Nissan sped down Highway 15, south toward California. Kelsey swore he would spend his wedding night as far away from his home as he could even though it would make for a longer drive the next day. Jordyn kept her eyes forward during the drive, her hand resting lightly on his thigh. Three times he asked if she was okay and, along with a reassuring smile, he got the same answer three times. She told him she couldn't be happier.

Kelsey, however, was a ball of muscle-bound nerves. He kept reminding himself to loosen his grip on the steering wheel. Keeping his thoughts on the road was also proving difficult due to the beautiful woman who was now his sitting quietly beside him.

Christ, he thought, *I feel like a virgin again.* A small wave of nausea flooded his stomach as he thought about how not a virgin he was. An even larger wave made him grip the steering wheel harder as he realized how not a virgin she was.

Moving on impulse, he let his foot off the gas pedal and pulled joltingly down a gravel side road into a low set of hills. She didn't say a word, but her hand tightened on his leg as the Nissan bumped over some particularly large rocks. The gravel road proved to be a short one and dead ended shortly after the highway disappeared behind one of the low barren hills. He cut the Nissan's engine and watched the dust settle on the windshield.

Well, he thought, *this is as good a campsite as any in this godforsaken desert. What kind of husband am I?* He chanced a look at his new bride.

Jordyn looked amused at his disheveled face, though she kept her mouth shut. Smoothing her dress over her thighs, she began to play with the hem.

Why doesn't she say anything? Kelsey wondered.

"Well. Is this okay?" His tone was harsher than he'd intended.

"Mm-hm," she spoke to her lap, lips still closed.

"Do you want to go farther?" He paused and waited, hoping that he sounded nicer than he felt. She didn't answer but he saw her shoulders shake.

His head came down to rest on the top of the steering wheel. His shoulders slumped over in defeat. "I'm so sorry, Darlin'. So, so sorry."

Her hand was quick to his back; her voice was choked but insistent. "No, Kels. No." Another garbled noise. "I just...I think it's funny, is all."

He jerked his head up to look at her face. It was red with suppressed laughter. He felt his brows come together and her laughter broke loose. She laughed until she gasped for air. He watched, transfixed by her odd mood.

When she calmed herself, he handed her a bottle of water and she drank deeply, a small stream of water falling from the side of her mouth onto her breast, the dark wet splotch growing until she set the bottle down. A small aftershock of laughter shook her before she finally looked him in the eyes.

"This is perfect." She grabbed his hand and gave it a reassuring squeeze. "It's just that nothing is going like I imagined it. And you are so cute when you are upset. And, well, all I can do is laugh. It's a hell of a lot better than crying right now." A giggle bubbled from her and she swallowed to stop it. "I know you are trying to make me happy." She squeezed again.

"Well, yea, I am!"

"You are," she replied.

"You don't want to keep going?"

"No, let's set up camp." She grabbed the door handle and hopped out of the car. The slam of the door closing was that of a final decision. He shook his head and followed her out.

...

They uncovered a place where there was evidence of a previous camp. There was a small round circle of stones containing the remains of old firewood and a level place to set up the small tent Jordyn had packed. It was hot in the desert sun; their clothes were soaked through within minutes. They mostly worked in silence, each thinking about the events of the day and the upcoming expectations of the night. Every few minutes they would catch each other's eye and smile; whether from nerves or anticipation, Kelsey didn't know.

The sky was streaks of orange, red and blue before they sat down to share a ham and swiss sandwich they had purchased at the last gas station. Even without fuel to start a campfire, they still sat around the circle of stones, peering into the long-extinguished pile of charred wood. The ground was warm beneath them, heated by the late-summer sun. A small breeze signaled the beginning of the evening and brought with it waves of welcomed coolness.

Kelsey looked up at Jordyn and watched her as she ate. Her white dress was now dirty from setting up camp in the desert. Her hair was wind-blown and her cheeks and lips were pink from the sun. Despite being dirty and tired in the middle of nowhere off a highway next to a dead campfire, he thought she couldn't be more beautiful. She looked back at him and the sun shone over her face, highlighting brown, blue and grey flecks among her green eyes, the skin around them creasing as she smiled.

"You didn't wear any makeup today," Kelsey said and watched her cheeks blush pinker as she glanced away.

"I just wanted to be me today," she said quietly, examining his face.

"I love it." Kelsey reached forward and put his hand on her knee. She rested her hand lightly on his, stroking his knuckles. "You are a beautiful woman."

"Right back at you," she said. She laughed. "I mean — man. But not beautiful — handsome. Oh, forget it." Kelsey joined in her laughter.

"I've never been called a beautiful woman before, but coming from you, I'll take it." He playfully brushed her shoulder with his own. She leaned her head against him.

They fell into silence, listening to each other's breathing. He could feel the heat from her head on his shoulder. It was a comforting weight, completely familiar and somehow new. Her hand continued to trace the lines of his fingers and knuckles. Every place she touched, his skin felt icy hot. An electric current began to flow through him, hungry and untamable. He rested his lips on the top of her head and felt his heart beat harder. Her hand froze over his.

"Kelsey." Just his name, spoken quietly into the sunset, lit him on fire.

Reaching around her, he gently turned her body to his. Her face shone up at him in the light of the setting sun, giving the illusion that she was on fire as well. He rested his head against her forehead and inhaled as she exhaled. Her breath was sweet, warm and intoxicating. He was vaguely aware that the tips of his fingers and toes were beginning to tingle. His hands pressed firm and wide into the small of her back. She arched toward him. As their lips met, the whole world exploded.

Bringing her face up to his, he stood up and grabbed both of her hands. He led her to the tent and onto the sleeping bags they had zipped together. They laughed as they struggled to kick their shoes off and fling them out into the desert night. The door caught as Kelsey tried to zip it up. He gave up after Jordyn stopped helping him with the door and started unbuttoning his shirt instead.

"God-damn door," he said and turned quickly to face Jordyn.

She was still unbuttoning his shirt, but, as her hands worked the buttons, she looked up into his face. Jordyn's eyes were a mix of gentleness, love, desire and apprehension. He had never seen a woman look that way before. And it was terribly attractive. He kissed her full lips and pulled her body close.

"Forgive me if I go too quickly," he whispered against her lips. He felt her smile.

"I can do that."

...

A wisp of downy soft hair tickled his chin. He reached to smooth it over her head, which was perfectly fitted into the space between his arm and chest. He could see the crest of her forehead, tip of her nose and swell of her lips glowing a cool blue from the moon overhead. Her hands were clasped together under her chin, grasping the edge of the sleeping bag that covered the rest of her body. He sighed softly, twirled the tendrils of her hair around his fingers, and looked through the crack in the door of the tent into the clear star-studded sky.

The night had started moonless, but they had been treated to a spectacular moon rise shortly after dark. It moon rose full and bright, sending its soft rays over the rocky land and low hills around them. No rock or sage brush was hidden from view in the vast desert though the landscape looked foreign in the strange light. Kelsey and Jordyn felt that they were living on a new planet. They felt that they had escaped from this world entirely, if only for the night.

He breathed in the scent of her hair, her skin and the primal smell of their lovemaking. He could feel her whole body pressed naked against his: head, breasts, belly, the tickle of hair above her legs, even her feet tangled with his. A shiver of remembering how they'd used their bodies just minutes before rippled over the skin on his thighs. He reached his mouth down to kiss her head. She tilted her face up and kissed him with her full lips, then lingered there, keeping her forehead and lips pressed lightly to his own. He felt one of her hands snake across his chest. She pulled him even closer to her body and held him tight.

They listened to the quiet purr of far-off highway noise mingled with the small rustlings of nighttime desert creatures. Now and then, the distant sound of a jet rose and fell above them. A small breeze blew both warm and cool through the tent walls. The longer they lay there, the more he wanted her again. Above the outside noises, he could hear his breathing slightly increase, faster and deeper. She heard it too. The sound of her body gliding through the nylon sleeping bag made the hair on his arms raise. Suddenly, the stars in the sky were blotted out by her naked form.

"Listen, Darlin'." His voice was hoarse and deep and he grasped her hands, which rested, fingers spread, over his chest. "Lord knows I want you again." He felt her wriggle slightly on his lap. "But if you're tired and all, I—I mean," he stuttered. "I don't want to make you feel like you have to...you know?" A warm finger pressed against his lips, effectively keeping him from speaking.

She leaned next to his ear and whispered, "I'll let you know the second I feel like I have to." Her teeth bit playfully on his earlobe and he squirmed a bit.

He was nearly unable to hold himself back from taking her again now. Her whole body was on fire and he felt like a match to the flame. Everywhere she touched him lit a fuse: her cheek, chest, breasts, thighs, even her feet. He had something he needed to say though, and he wanted to say it before he lost himself.

He grabbed her hands, which were migrating down his body and dangerously close to the point of no return.

"Darlin'," he said firmly, holding her hands tight, restraining her from moving farther. She made a noncommittal noise and looked up at him through dark lashes, eyes glowing grey blue in the moonlight. "Jordyn," he said, feeling urgent.

"Yes?" She smirked and bit her lip as she tried to wriggle free of his grasp, inching back toward her goal.

"I need to say something." He felt her hands reluctantly relax.

"M'kay," she said, and rested her head on his chest.

"Can I look at you?"

She looked up at him again and, after he had freed her hand, propped herself up on an elbow, waiting expectantly. "Go ahead."

"I love you."

The words hung in the air between them, almost taking a physical shape, a balloon ready to pop. She stared at him, searching his face. She blinked and he saw tears glisten in her eyes just before she buried her face in his chest. Her shoulders began to shake and he both felt and heard stifled sobs against him. He pulled her closer, arms wound snuggly around her back and held tight. Her sobs turned to soft crying and eventually faded into intakes of jerky breath.

She shifted herself to his side, keeping her head against his shoulder. He stroked her hair soothingly. Kelsey didn't know why his words had caused such a powerful reaction, but he'd meant them and felt they'd been important to say at that moment.

"Thank you," she whispered from under his chin, her breath tickling the hair at the top of his chest.

"I mean it," he replied.

"I know." Another quick inhale and a deep breath. "It's just... No one's ever said that to me while..." She paused. "And... Oh, Kels, I do love you so much." She turned her head into his shoulder and began to cry again.

"Shh. I know, Darlin'. I know." Kelsey felt as if his heart would burst from his chest, whether from pain or the love he felt for her, he didn't know. He felt a great racking breath fill his lungs and he held it to keep from dissolving.

His insides were a mix of dark and light, midnight and noon, oil and water. How could he feel such heartbreak, pain and disappointment while loving this woman with everything that he was? He hated the decision she'd felt she'd had to make to be a prostitute. He hated that she had lied to him. He hated that she had been treated like shit; but god, he loved the woman herself. He couldn't even articulate why he loved her so much. He just did.

As she quietly cried into his shoulder and he lay trying to regain control, a thought floated to the surface of his churning mind. He saw her Bible as he had seen it the first time, lying in his lap after it had fallen out of her backpack. The strange vision of her Bible reminded him of the God she had described and professed her love for earlier this weekend.

Was this love he felt for Jordyn what she meant when she described her God hating the shitty stuff she did but loving her anyway?

He'd never thought of God that way; but there it was — a thought, unbidden, resting snuggly in a corner of his mind in the way her head rested on his shoulder.

He looked down on her, realizing she had stopped crying and that he had regained control of his roiling insides. He looked up through the mesh roof of the tent and watched a slow-moving satellite on a suicide mission into the full moon. He imagined it splashing into the moon's surface the way a small rock would into a lake. He looked back to Jordyn and found her eyes on his face, a small smile on her lips.

"I'm sorry," she said.

"Don't be."

"It's our wedding night. And I'm crying because you told me you loved me." She giggled nervously through a small hic-cup.

"There's nothing that could ruin this night," Kelsey replied. "Nothing."

He stroked her bare back. He moved his hand up and down from her shoulders to the base of her spine. She sighed and snuggled in close. A twinge in his groin reminded him of what they had been doing before he'd told her he loved her. He tried to turn his body away so that she didn't notice, but it was too late.

"Just because I was crying doesn't mean you are off the hook," she said into his neck, sending shivers all the way down his back. Her lips pressed along his jawbone and chin, finally landing on his own lips.

"I still don't want you to feel like you have to..." The same warm finger pressed his lips closed.

"What did I say before, Kelsey Campbell?" The smile was back in her voice. "I will let you know."

Her hands moved down his body, exploring. Her breasts pressed soft and warm into his arm. Her lips traveled across his neck, tracing a cool line around his face. This time, when she reached down and found her goal, he didn't try to stop her.

Chapter 18

THE GLOW FROM THEIR faces matched the light of the sun rising over the desert. Kelsey couldn't remember feeling this content in his whole life. From the look on Jordyn's face, she felt the same. Their happiness continued to grow with the sun's ascension into the midday sky.

Jordyn helped him pack the tent and their bags in the car. She kissed his cheek, lingering there and sending tingles to the tips of his toes.

"Thank you for last night...and last night...and this morning," she whispered into his ear, this time sending tingles through his groin.

"You're welcome...you're welcome...and you're welcome," he said. She giggled. He pulled her close and whispered into her ear. "Thank you." He felt her cheek rise into a smile against his lips.

The world slipped by outside the windows of the Nissan as they drove north. Kelsey felt invincible as he held Jordyn's hand on his knee. He couldn't be more in love. He wanted to feel this close to her always, to know her inside and out. He cast a quick grin at her, feeling reckless.

"Alright, tell me more about your Bible."

Jordyn looked at him, shocked. "Kelsey, you didn't take too well to our last conversation."

"I know. But I'm in a much better mood now." He squeezed her hand. "And I want to know what makes you tick."

She pursed her lips, thinking before deciding to continue. "Alright. What do you want to know?"

This made him pause. He wasn't really sure what he wanted to know. He decided honesty was his only option. "I don't know." He felt her staring at the side of his face. "I mean, you seem real happy when you talk about it. You said you found real love." He fished for words. "Last night, I...was thinking about it. And, I think I understand what you meant about God loving you despite all the shit. But, what then? Life is still fucked up. Nothing changes. What's the point?" Kelsey realized his voice had risen. He cleared his throat to hide the emotion that had gathered there.

Jordyn squinted her eyes at him, gauging his mood. She turned her face forward and sat in silence for a thoughtful moment. "Everything changes," she said. "In the Bible, there is a story about a prostitute who comes to Jesus. She comes to him because she recognizes him as the person who would offer her an escape from her immoral life. She pours a bottle of expensive perfume on Jesus's feet. She lets down her hair and starts to wipe Jesus's feet with it." Jordyn grinned at the look on Kelsey's face. "I know, sounds gross right? And everyone around Jesus didn't think too much of what she did either. They didn't think much of the prostitute herself. But Jesus explains to them that the woman was so overcome with gratefulness for who He was and what He offered that she basically poured herself out in thanks to Him. Jesus explained that people who have a lot to be forgiven for are more thankful than those who don't think they have much to be forgiven for." Jordyn glanced at Kelsey. "Jesus told the prostitute she was saved."

Kelsey thought for a moment. "Okay, but you still didn't answer my question. What then? She's still a prostitute."

"Do you really think she went back to her old life after that? Do you think she continued to live in a way that she knew God didn't like? After completely pouring herself out in front of all those people with no fear of what would come? I don't think so, Kels. Can't you see that her life would fundamentally be changed? She would forever live in awe and gratefulness. She wouldn't need to whore. Because, no matter the consequences, she couldn't continue to live in a way that made Jesus unhappy...even if it meant death. She was given something infinitely more valuable than her life. She was given freedom and liberation."

Kelsey remained silent, processing. The sage and desert dust blurred on the periphery of his vision as the center markings on the road ticked by.

"The prostitute was that grateful even before she knew that Jesus would die to save her one day." Jordyn paused for a few breaths. "Kels, I am that woman. Those words Jesus spoke that day were about me. Then Jesus died...for me. Don't you see? Everything changes."

Kelsey's top teeth worked his bottom lip. Jordyn's breathing was even and peaceful by his side. A flicker of what she said rang true somewhere in his gut, but he couldn't shake the feeling that he was missing something big. The sensation of incomplete understanding was making him uncomfortable. It churned in his belly and made him feel irritable. He felt the familiar tingle of tension in his muscles.

He didn't want to fight Jordyn though. He let the tranquility that flowed in an electric current from her body sooth his nerves. He reached for her hand and took a cleansing breath.

She smiled at him, face beaming. He couldn't help but smile back.

Her love of Jesus and that Bible was not an issue he was going to fully understand soon. He was going to have to get used to the feeling that he was missing something. But looking at her sitting next to him, hand in his, he knew he could be patient for this woman. After all, she was right so far — love had been enough. And god, he loved her so.

The rest of their drive was spent laughing, cuddling and enjoying each other's presence. By the time they passed through the familiar sites of Beatty, Kelsey felt invincible once again and ready for anything.

He spotted his sister's dark green Dodge Neon as soon as they turned from the highway into his driveway. His heart skipped with excitement. Jordyn smiled at him. He couldn't wait to introduce her to Anne.

Darkness shadowed his sunny excitement when he noted that Brad's truck was at home too. He grimly hoped Brad was passed out in his room.

"It's going to be great," Jordyn said, apparently reading his mind. "I'm so happy I get to meet her. And forget about Brad."

Kelsey forced a reassuring smile.

Damn Brad to hell, he thought. *It will be great.*

...

The front door slammed open against the side of the house with a loud bang then swung shut with a quiet thud. Kelsey craned his neck to look inside for his sister, expectantly waiting to see her round pink face, mischievous smile and dark tangle of curls running to meet him. Instead, his eyes rested on the back of Brad's head, disheveled brown hair poking straight up where it was matted down from sleep. Brad was facing away from Kelsey, seated in his recliner. It was eerily quiet in the room that was usually filled with the boisterous sound of the television.

Something was very wrong. Kelsey's heart thumped hard.

Brad's hand rested on the table next to the recliner. Cupped casually in it was a .45 caliber revolver. Next to the revolver sat an empty bottle of whiskey. Kelsey froze, eyes locked on the gun and the whiskey.

Whiskey, he thought, *not whiskey.*

Kelsey felt his hand twitch up to his forehead. His fingers lightly smoothed over the faded scar above his right eye. A lifelong reminder of Brad and what he was capable of. His mouth went dry and his eardrums started to buzz with adrenaline.

Stop, he thought, *there's no time for that. No time for fear.*

"Where the hell is Anne?" Kelsey heard his own voice as if outside his body. His tone was cool, deep and clipped.

He saw Brad's hand twitch over the .45.

"I'm going to ask one more time... Where is my sister?" Kelsey watched Brad's fingers squeeze tight around the .45's handle. Kelsey clenched his own fists and flexed his thighs. It took all of his self-control to keep from jumping on Brad's back and wrestling the gun out of his hand.

"Get out of here, Son." Brads voice was gravelly and slurred. "Go take your little whore of a girlfriend and get out of here."

Oh god, Kelsey moaned internally and his stomach flipped over. *Jordyn.* She was going to grab a couple things from the trunk of the Nissan and follow him in. *Stay out, stay out*, he silently begged her.

Seizing on an idea, he reached behind him and locked the door. The cool metal of the deadbolt slid quietly into place. He took a small breath of relief.

Brad leaned forward in his chair, back still to Kelsey, putting his elbows on his knees and resting the barrel of the gun to his forehead. Kelsey could hear him breathing now, rough and fast. Kelsey glanced around the small living room, grasping at anything that might help him. The room was dim. Hazy light shone through the curtains, orange and yellow in the thick air. The worn brown couch across the room was empty. Next to it, a dark mass on the ground caught his eye.

A body.

"Anne!" Kelsey's voice broke and he took an involuntary step forward. At the same time, Brad stood and whirled, swaying precariously on shaky legs as he held the gun, casually aiming it at Kelsey. Kelsey took another involuntary step backward and held his hands open to his sides. He looked frantically behind Brad, fear and hate beginning to bubble inside him.

Oh god, Anne! His heart cried out and his stomach lurched.

She lay on her stomach beside the couch, black curly hair spilling around her blank face. Her eyes were closed and her cheek was pressed hard against the dark green shag carpet. He couldn't see if she was breathing or not. Squinting his eyes in the dimness, he tried to see if there were any signs of life. As he became accustomed to the light, he sucked a sharp breath through his teeth. A slick dark liquid was pooling under Anne's cheek and through the hair that was matted on the carpet. He looked back at Brad, eyes burning black now, as black as his father's.

"You know," Brad said, his words too slurred and too loud for the small space, "I used to think you were just like her. Your momma, I mean." The gun swung back and forth through the room. "But now...now I know you are just like me." His mouth turned into a half smile, revealing a bloody upper lip and teeth. Had Anne injured him?

"I used to wonder if you were even mine, or if that bitch just forced herself and her damn baby on me. But now! Yes, now I know." Brad smiled again and rested the back of the gun against the side of his head. "That pretty little whore of yours," he went on. "Truth is, I can't see why you follow her around like a little puppy dog. Skinny little body and big ears. She must be pretty damn good in bed, eh? Your momma wasn't much to look at either, but man was she a good fuck."

Kelsey clenched his fists harder, digging his nails into his palms, waiting for the right moment. The right moment for what, he didn't know.

"Has your whore forced a baby on you too?" Brad continued and laughed at the anger that shown plain on Kelsey's face. "Yes? Well, see then?" His next words were accentuated and clear. "You are just...like...me." He laughed again; a drop of saliva shot from his mouth and landed on his stubbled chin. "You know what? Do them a favor and kill her now. It'll save you from having to kill them both after the bastard has been born."

Kelsey sucked in a steady breath. His eyes flicked back and forth over his father's large frame. What was Brad saying?

"Surprised, Son? Why? You are just like me. Don't tell me you haven't thought of it." Brad waved the gun at Kelsey. "Trust me, I've often thought I should've killed her while you were still a parasite in her cursed belly. It would've saved me the trouble of twenty-one fucked-up years. Yea, I should've stuck her with that needle years before."

Kelsey's eyes widened, a sickening understanding of what Brad had said washing over his tense body. Brad had killed his mom. He was the one who had overdosed her.

Brad continued and Kelsey watched him in horror. "I'm so glad Delilah showed up here today." A horrific grin transformed Brad's face.

Delilah? Kelsey's mind worked to put the pieces together. Kelsey's eyes moved in slow motion to his sister lying on the floor. *That's not Anne's mom. That's not Delilah... Oh god, Brad thought Anne was Delilah.*

He killed her.

Just like he killed my mom.

A light rap on the door sent a lightning bolt through his spine and shocked him from his thoughts. Brad jumped too, his finger twitching precariously on the trigger.

"Who's that?" Brad asked. A flicker of fear passed over his brow.

"Nobody," Kelsey said through gritted teeth. He had to get to Brad before Jordyn found her way in.

"Ah, it's the little brown-headed whore!" Brad grinned again. "Go on, let her in."

"No," Kelsey growled.

Brad's smile widened.

He squeezed the trigger.

The bullet hit the wall behind Kelsey, tearing a hole in the faux wood paneling. A muffled cry sounded from outside the door.

"Kelsey?" Jordyn's voice sounded surprised.

And unhurt.

Kelsey dove.

The force of their bodies colliding felt like driving into a brick wall at 60 miles per hour. Despite the impact, neither man fell to the ground. They embraced in a deadly bear hug, each trying to topple the other. Kelsey's had the advantage of youth and sound body, but Brad's leathery tenacity and numbness from drink kept him going.

Kelsey felt Brad's arm flex behind him.

The gun went off again.

A searing pain split the back of Kelsey's head. He convulsively released Brad and stumbled toward the couch, fighting the blackness that attempted to overcome him. He vaguely heard Jordyn's frantic voice calling his name. He fell to one knee, inches from his sister's immobile body. Her blood soaked into the fabric of his knee. He reached for her, his vision swimming. Her dark locks were slick and damp with blood.

Jordyn shouted from outside again. Kelsey swiveled clumsily on his knee, unable to stand due to the pounding pain, helpless to get to her. Brad stood staring at Kelsey and his sister with a vacant expression. Brad looked down at the gun in his hand.

Kelsey felt himself being pulled into black weightlessness. The sides of his vision undulated and blurred. His throat and chest ached to scream at Jordyn, to tell her to get away, but his body betrayed him. His limbs felt trapped in sand, willing but unable to move.

Brad continued to study the gun in his hand. In a last attempt to get to him, Kelsey lunged forward. He fell to his hands and both knees, losing his fight against the darkness that pulled him. With great effort he moved to look at Brad again. His blurred vision focused just long enough to see Brad lift the gun barrel into his mouth.

The room sparked and exploded in sound and color.

Kelsey collapsed and knew no more.

Chapter 19

KELSEY TIGHTLY PRESSED his eyes shut and pretended to be somewhere else. It didn't work. The low murmuring of a respirator and the faint beep-beep of a heart monitor mirrored his own inhalations and heartbeat. Dry cool air filtered into his lungs, smelling of astringent rubbing alcohol and hand soap. He was in a hospital, and no amount of fantasizing would change that.

He looked through a half-open eye at his sister. She didn't know where she was. She didn't have to suffer the recirculated air and taste cafeteria food. She didn't have to worry or wonder if one of the two closest people in her life was going to die. Pain mingled with jealousy as he watched her sleeping peacefully on the partially raised cot.

Under his thumb, he felt the gentle throbbing of Anne's pulse in her wrist. He sighed. It had been three weeks. During all that time, her pulse and the slight rise and fall of her chest were the only signs she was still alive.

Jordyn told Kelsey that when the paramedics arrived after he passed out, Anne had opened her eyes for a moment. They fluttered and quickly closed again as she fell back into unconsciousness. That was the last time they saw Anne move.

Kelsey had gone to the hospital by ambulance after his sister, though he didn't remember it. The bullet that Brad fired had grazed the back of Kelsey's head, causing a lot of blood loss, along with a temporary loss of consciousness. Unlike his sister, Kelsey was allowed to leave his hospital bed within 24 hours, heavily bandaged but otherwise intact.

The doctor had done an initial CT scan on Anne three weeks ago. They'd found severe brain trauma and swelling from the bullet that Brad had fired through her skull. The doctors placed her in a medically induced coma and kept her in the intensive care unit for observation and treatment. They told Kelsey and Jordyn that the only definitive treatment was to see if she would wake up after the swelling went down. In the meantime, they were treating her by placing a shunt into her skull to drain fluid. In addition to the shunt, she was on a slew of medications, most of which Kelsey couldn't dream of pronouncing. He had no knowledge of medical procedures, and was left to trust the doctors and hospital staff with his sister's life.

The doctor in charge of Anne's case was a middle-aged, generic type of man, medium height and build, dark haired, with a prominent nose being his only distinguishing feature. He told Kelsey to call him Sam, though he heard the nurses call him Dr. Russo. Dr. Sam Russo had ordered an MRI for Anne earlier, and had told Kelsey the MRI would give them a better picture of her brain and potentially help determine her long-term prognosis. It had been an hour and they were waiting on the results.

Kelsey had stayed with Anne every moment since her arrival at the hospital, leaving only for an occasional meal in the cafeteria or to shower. He slept next to her bed, was there for every update, and watched vigilantly for a flutter of her eyelids. Jordyn was also there for the first two weeks, occasionally breaking away to care for Lizzie. After two weeks of no change, Jordyn started to pick up a few shifts at the market.

The weight of worry was heavy and distracting. Jordyn and Kelsey's conversations were disjointed and superficial. They shared a few brief smiles, and chaste kisses, and held each other tightly in the moments when life was too heavy. They drew strength from each other, though neither was prepared for the gravity of the situation.

No one else visited Anne because there was no one. Kelsey didn't have the contact information for Anne's mom and guessed that she'd be too high to understand or care about what was happening. Anne's room was devoid of cards or teddy bears. Kelsey saw flowers in many of the other hospital rooms, and so he bought a small bunch of artificially colored daisies at the gift shop on the first floor of the hospital. He put them in a cup next to the head of her bed. The flowers looked small and pitiful next to his sister. Eventually, he'd moved them to the window, where they now sat wilting.

The soft sound of the door pushing open and clicking shut registered behind his closed eyelids. The weight of the last few restless nights was carrying him into sleep, so he didn't bother opening his eyes to see who'd entered. Jordyn had left for work a few hours ago, so it must be another nurse doing her hourly rounds. He listened as soft shoes padded up to the bed. He heard the muffled rustling of Anne's pillow as it was adjusted and then more muted steps. Soft lips pressed to his cheek. His eyes sprang open in surprise.

The fuzzy outline of Jordyn's face surrounded by a cloud of brightly illuminated brown hair took form in front of him. His lips parted in a sleepy smile. He closed his eyes again and pulled her onto his lap, letting his feet fall to the ground from their resting place on the side of Anne's bed. Jordyn's weight was solid, warm and comforting on his thighs. Had it really been since the night they were married that he had touched her body, really touched it? And had it really been only three weeks ago? It felt longer, if it had even happened at all. He sighed as she leaned into him, pressing her cheek to his forehead.

"I thought you were going to be at work, Darlin,'" Kelsey said quietly into her ear, not wanting to fully wake.

"I was. The store was slow this afternoon. I asked to go." Her tone was quiet, mirroring his. The breath from her mouth tickled the loose hair on his head. "I thought you looked like you could use more company when I left you earlier." She reached up and ran her fingers lightly over the back of his head.

"Mmm." Kelsey's voice was husky with sleep. "I always need more of your company." He playfully squeezed her butt, causing her to squirm. He smiled, feeling her silent giggle against his hair.

"No change?" she asked after a moment.

"Nothing," he answered, feeling a frown wrinkle the space between his eyebrows. She kissed it.

"I'll let you sleep. I'm going to stay here for a while so I'll keep an eye on her." She kissed his open lips, squeezed his hand, and her weight lifted from his lap. Kelsey opened an eye and gave her a half smile.

"Thanks. Just give me a few minutes."

...

He woke to the sound of the nurse bustling into the room for her hourly rounds. He could tell by the light outside that he had slept for hours instead of minutes. The sun was sinking low in the sky, casting a fiery orange glow around the room. He arched his cramped spine and kneaded a tight muscle in the side of his neck.

It was the nurse he liked. She had a pleasant round face with sparkling blue eyes atop an expansive bosom and even more expansive body; Karen, he thought her name was. She smiled at him and he readily returned it.

When the sleep cleared from his eyes he looked at Anne. Karen was lifting Anne's arm to see that the blood pressure cuff was properly placed. The orange light from the sinking sun gave Anne's face a healthy glow. It lit the tousled black curls that were strewn haphazardly on the pillow behind her. Her eyelids glowed faintly purple over thick black lashes. She had perfect skin, almost translucent in its smoothness. Though her skin was pale, the sun made it shine. She was so beautiful and so young. He briefly touched Anne's wrist, almost unconsciously moving his fingers to the place where the base of her thumb met the crease of her wrist, checking her pulse. He watched the familiar rise and fall of her chest. No changes, but for the moment that was a comfort.

Kelsey then focused on Jordyn. She was sitting in a straight-backed chair, her feet up on the side of Anne's bed. Her long pale legs shone golden in the light. She had the leather-bound Bible open on her lap. He watched her read. Her lips moved, her brow sometimes furrowed as she considered the words she was reading. She was biting the corners of her fingernails, something he had noticed her doing whenever she thought hard. The nurse set a metal tray of IV supplies noisily on the counter and startled Jordyn. She glanced up from her reading and met Kelsey's eyes. A wide smile immediately transformed her contemplative features.

"You're up," she said soothingly.

"Eh?" Karen looked up from sorting her equipment and glanced at Kelsey, then at Jordyn. "Oh, I'm almost done. Don't mind me, Sweets." Her endearing term caused them to grin.

"Take your time," Kelsey said. "Any news?"

"I'm sorry, Hon," Karen replied. "Nothing new this afternoon." A little sparkle lit her eyes and she said, "I've never told you what a beautiful lady you have here." She nodded at Jordyn.

He gave her a shy smile. "Sure do, Karen. Thank you."

She smiled and bobbed her head in acknowledgment, picked up the tray and moved briskly out the open door, pushing it closed behind her with the back of her foot. The door clicked shut.

Kelsey reached both arms up in the air and stretched. With a huge yawn he scooted back in his chair and sat up straight. Jordyn watched him.

"What?" he asked, squinting his eyes conspiratorially.

"Nothin'," she replied, her own eyes narrowing with her smile.

"How long was I out?"

"Maybe an hour and a half. You feel better?"

"I do." And he did. The fog of tiredness was gone, at least for the moment.

Maybe it was the magic of the setting sun, the peaceful rest or the presence of Jordyn, but he felt like he could really breathe for the first time in weeks. He felt the need to stand up and move.

He walked to the window. Five stories below, cars drove around in the parking lot. Farther out, the desert stretched for miles until it ran into low hills. The hills were backlit by the huge glowing orb of sunlight. He couldn't look straight at it.

Something about the light reminded him of the afternoon in Vegas when he and Jordyn had walked to the Chapel of Rock n' Roll. He remembered standing on the stage with Elvis, nervous as hell, and pledging himself to her. His heart swelled with joyful remembrance.

He caught the reflection of his sister lying on the bed behind him. His joy quickly deflated as he contrasted his present with his not too distant past. The window of the hospital room suddenly felt like a prison.

It was so simple that day in Vegas — just Jordyn and Kelsey, wildly passionate and wanting more than life to be joined for life. He had put his past behind him. He had forgiven Jordyn. He had forgotten the hopelessness of his damn town. He had forgotten Brad.

Oh god, Brad. Kelsey's throat tightened and his vision blurred hazy red as he thought of his father, but he brushed the thought of him aside as quickly as he could, not wanting to spiral into black thoughts, dark as the impending moonless night. The darkness lurked in the corners of his mind, however, ready to claim even more of him than it already had. Grasping for the joy he had just felt, he clung to that day in Vegas when their life together had seemed full of promises of light and love and freedom.

Since then, he had all but forgotten about the plans he'd had for his life. He'd forgotten about saving money for the 1981 Mustang Cobra. He'd forgotten about his job at the shop with Steve. He'd forgotten about Jordyn's job and her sister, Lizzie. He'd forgotten the joy he felt being with them. His old life seemed a distant memory. He would give anything to have it back. He would give anything to get back what Brad had stolen from him.

The little bit of rest he took was proving to be bittersweet. He had more energy, but also more capacity to think. A familiar white-hot anger started its usual course down the back of his neck and flowed through his veins to his fingertips.

It hadn't done any good not to think of Brad. The anger took hold anyway. Kelsey flexed his fingers and shrugged his shoulders, trying to rid himself of the rage that had fueled his life before Jordyn. Not succeeding, he brought his fist to the window in a controlled punching motion, barely letting his knuckles graze the cold glass. A grim smile moved the corners of his mouth. He was still in control of his body. His thoughts were another matter.

"Kels." Jordyn's soft voice brought him back to the present. He didn't turn to her, not wanting his face to betray his inward struggle. "Kels. Is everything okay?" He heard her steps behind him. Her gentle arms snaked around his middle, hands spreading over the t-shirt covering his stomach. He felt his muscles stiffen and then relax at her touch. He leaned his forearms on the window and his head onto his closed fists. The cold glass felt good, distracting.

"You don't have to answer that," Jordyn said. Her thumb stroked soothingly over the center of his breast bone. Her head rested lightly between his shoulder blades.

"I was just thinking about Vegas," Kelsey said after a moment.

"That bad, huh?" Her tone was light and joking, but her hands stilled while she waited for his response.

Kelsey snorted. "That good." Jordyn waited for him to go on. He took his time, not wanting to lose control. "So good. And this..."

He felt her head readjust on his back and her hands resumed their tiny movements on his chest. Her voice vibrated the center of his spine. "Yea. I know."

Kelsey felt himself relax a bit further. She did know. She knew as well as anyone how awful life could be. He'd seen her through nearly the worst life could throw, and she'd handled it without ever losing herself or losing the peace she claimed came from her Bible.

"How do you do it, Darlin'? How do you keep it together? I want to tear this room apart." Kelsey's hands clenched hard under his forehead. "Someone needs to pay for what happened to Anne. Brad ended his fucking life, so he can't pay. Someone needs to pay."

He felt Jordyn's even breathing on his back. "I think..." She paused, considering. "I think I can have hope and peace because someone did pay."

Kelsey wasn't expecting this. And it sounded as if Jordyn hadn't expected it either. He waited, unsure if she wanted him to answer.

"He did pay. For all this," she said. Her voice was wondering and reverential. She held still behind him.

Kelsey was confused. "Brad paid? Brad's dead. The son of a bitch got away with it."

Jordyn ignored the venom that oozed from Kelsey's words. Her tone was confident now. "Jesus paid."

Her two words hung in the air, stunning Kelsey again. He took a deep breath and let it out in defeat. "Oh, Jordyn."

Three weeks of sleepless nights and roiling emotions washed over him, causing him to physically slump. He was drained of all fight. He couldn't discuss it with her. She didn't seem to need to talk any more. She pulled him tight against her and rested her head on his back.

The doctor entered and startled them both from their thoughts. Jordyn released Kelsey's waist and they turned to face Dr. Russo, reaching for each other's hand, squeezing lightly. Dr. Russo held a chart tightly in his hand as he glanced first at Anne's monitor, then at her face, then finally to meet Kelsey's gaze.

"Doctor," Kelsey said with a nod.

"Good Evening, Mr. Campbell, Mrs. Campbell." Dr. Russo nodded back. "Have a seat." He motioned to the bench seat in front of the window. Kelsey and Jordyn sat down obediently. Dr. Russo sat on a rolling stool in front of them.

"We got the results of the MRI." As Dr. Russo spoke, Kelsey felt his chest tighten and still. "There is really no nice way to say this, Kelsey. Anne's brain swelling is increasing. We've done all we can for her but the swelling is beginning to press on her brain stem, which is causing brain death. The specialists and I have agreed that she has less than 24 hours to live."

Dr. Russo paused. Kelsey heard a soft cry from Jordyn and felt her hand tighten on his as he stared at Dr. Russo's face, focusing on his nose.

"I'm sorry, Mr. Campbell. Do you have any questions for me?" Dr. Russo's voice was gentle.

"No, Doctor. I don't," Kelsey heard himself say. Jordyn was crying softly into his arm.

Dr. Russo stood and placed a heavy hand on Kelsey's shoulder. "The nurse can get ahold of me anytime if you have questions. Again, I'm sorry." When Kelsey did not reply, Dr. Russo nodded. "I'll leave you together. Karen should be in for her rounds in fifteen minutes."

Kelsey didn't hear Dr. Russo leave. He didn't hear Jordyn crying at his side or the sounds of the machines around him. His eyes found Anne's face, peaceful as a child's in sleep. Without conscious thought he stood, letting Jordyn fall away from his arm, and walked to Anne's side. He sat down next to her on the cot and placed a hand over her heart. It beat as soft as a bird's wing under his palm.

The setting sun shone burnt orange on her face and throat. Her tousled curls fluttered around her face with each of her shallow exhales. He stroked a thumb over her freckled cheek. As he moved over the hollow under her cheek bone, the sun dipped below the distant hills, leaving her face in grey shadow. The loss of the sun was the loss of Kelsey's control. The weight of Anne's prognosis had shattered his heart. He lay down next to his sister and wept.

Chapter 20

ANNE'S BODY WAS STRONG and her spirit that of a fighter. So, what the doctors predicted would happen in twenty-four hours took forty-eight. Forty-eight long hours in which Kelsey and Jordyn never left her side. They slept for brief moments in their chairs and nibbled on the food offered by the nurses.

The majority of the last hours they spent with Anne were peaceful. While Anne didn't show any signs of wakefulness or understanding, she also didn't show any signs of suffering. The doctors said if Kelsey or Jordyn wanted to talk to Anne that they should lean close to her ear and speak. Kelsey doubted Anne would really hear him, but it felt good to tell her how much he loved her. Kelsey and Jordyn rarely spoke to each other, the heaviness of grief stealing their words.

The doctors warned them that the end might not be peaceful, and they were right. After the forty-seventh hour, the increasing swelling in Anne's brain and the ensuing pressure on her spinal column caused Anne to have seizures. Her body twitched and thrashed; her facial features distorted. Kelsey and Jordyn called for the nurse, trying to keep their hands on Anne's writhing body, but in the minute it took the nurse to arrive, the seizures ended. Anne's features fell slack and the whisper of a final breath escaped her parted lips.

Kelsey distantly registered that the monitor next to the bed softly whistled and a straight orange line worked its way across the screen. He fell over his sister and wrapped his arms around her body. It felt thin and as light as a bird's, as if she could fly away. He buried his face into the curls around her face. Jordyn wrapped Kelsey's body in her arms, her own body trembling. The tears came silently, trickling through Anne's hair and staining the pillow.

...

The nurses took pity on Kelsey and Jordyn, knowing they hadn't slept in days. They set up a cot in an empty hospital room and allowed them to sleep as long as the room wasn't needed. Much as they wanted to leave the hospital that had been their prison for three weeks, they couldn't deny that they needed the rest more.

Kelsey and Jordyn immediately fell asleep, but Kelsey woke to look at his watch every hour. Jordyn stirred restlessly next to him. Each time he woke and before he could convince himself to get up, his body fell back into an agitated slumber. After seven hours of this, he woke again. Groaning, he checked his watch. It was 5 pm, of what day he didn't know. He glanced over to check if Jordyn was awake but found the cot beside him empty.

The long hall outside the hospital room was buzzing with life. Nurses carried trays and pushed carts from room to room, patients wandered between them, and a few doctors stood reading charts. The lights and sounds were overwhelming to Kelsey, who still didn't feel fully awake. He aimed himself at the desk halfway down the hall, intending to ask if anyone had seen Jordyn.

He spotted her not far from the desk. From ten yards away, he could see her smile. It lit up the hallway. Her smile wasn't for Kelsey though. A doctor, distinguishable due to his blue lab jacket and shiny leather shoes, stood across from her, a thin smile on his lips. Something about the way Jordyn was looking at him made Kelsey stop dead in the center of the hall. She was leaning back, one foot drawn up and pressed against the wall behind her. She reached up to push a strand of hair behind her ear and smile up at the doctor. He said something that made her laugh. The doctor was casual, conversational and too familiar.

Kelsey's vision blurred as he watched them. An image of Jordyn and the doctor falling together in a passionate lover's embrace jumped vividly to his mind. The doctor's hands caressed her body; his face pressed to hers. She melted into him, running her fingers through his hair. Kelsey blinked. The two figures separated. His vision cleared, leaving behind white-hot rage.

His sister lay cold and dead in the morgue below them. His new wife was selling herself to a doctor while he slept.

A low growl rose from his chest. His teeth ground together. His muscles twitched to move. At that moment, Jordyn glanced in his direction. Her eyes lit and she waved. Kelsey felt his feet carry him closer. The light in Jordyn's eyes faltered when she saw his face. She reached out to touch his arm and he jerked it away. She frowned, but caught sight of the doctor and regained her lightness. She reached to hold the doctor's arm. Kelsey's gaze locked on her face, blinded by red fire.

"Kelsey!" Her voice was bright and quick. "I want you to meet Lizzie's cardiologist. We were talking cars and he is selling his daughter's 1981 Mustang Cobra! Aren't you—"

"What the fuck, Jordyn?" Kelsey's entire body vibrated, his voice a dull roar in his ears. Her words had fallen on rage-deaf ears. "This guy?"

Jordyn's face fell into wounded shock. Her hand gripped the doctor's sleeve. "Kelsey?" Confusion and pain transformed her features. Her hand fell away from the doctor's arm.

"Kelsey..."

The sound of her voice saying his name died behind him as he spun and barreled for the neon green exit sign. The hall carried him by the room his sister had occupied. He stumbled sideways as he caught sight of the bed. Fresh memories of her death just hours ago brought stinging tears to his eyes. He caught himself on the wall and launched himself forward again.

No one followed him through the exit doors and into the parking lot. The '92 roared to life, vibrating his thighs as he sped the truck onto the highway.

Blind rage numbed his senses better than any drink, but he stopped at the market anyway. Half a fifth of tequila on an exhausted and empty stomach was enough to cripple a man, but Kelsey had been practicing for this for years.

The '92 sped north, a neon pink sign glowing promisingly ahead.

Chapter 21

THE WORN SURFACE OF the wooden bar was warm and smooth under Kelsey's cheek. The glass cradled in his hand refracted Coors Light–colored flecks of light onto his forearm. Blurry shapes moved slowly beyond the glass and muffled voices echoed in the air around his ears. A trickle of drool inched its way down the corner of his mouth and onto the wooden surface below. The cheek pressed against the bar pushed against his flaccid lips, causing them to protrude. One eye was open and gazed dreamily through the glass.

A whoosh, a change in air pressure and a thud alerted him that the door to the brothel had opened. He hiccupped and closed his one open eye.

"Can I help you, Darlin'?" a woman's voice spoke over his head. It was familiar to him, but he couldn't remember the woman's name.

Is her name Cherry?

"I think you already are." Another woman's voice behind him. This one was familiar too. Very familiar. The eye opened again. His torso twitched on the bar stool.

"How you doing, Steve?" The first woman spoke — *is her name Chelsie?* "You did a fine job on my Taurus. It runs like a dream."

"I'm glad it's working out, Charity." A man's voice this time.

Her name is Charity...

"How long has he been here?" The man spoke again. His boss — Steve. Kelsey lifted his head two inches at the sound of his boss's voice.

"Mmm, a couple hours," Charity said from somewhere near his ear. "I gotta tell you, Steve, I wasn't excited to see him come in because of the way he acted last time he was here. But he seemed pretty harmless tonight. Sad almost. He sat down, asked for a drink and paid me twenty bucks to let him touch my tits. Afterward he laid his head down on the bar there. I just let him be. I don't have any other customers tonight so it's been alright."

Kelsey lifted his upper body enough to move his head onto his forearms. Two naked breasts hovered inches from his cheek. He collapsed on the bar again.

"That's kind of you, Charity. His sister passed away today." Steve's subdued voice came from beside Kelsey's head, causing him to flinch.

"Oh, I'm sorry to hear it. The girls and I were really pulling for her to come out of it. I was glad to see the community come together to put in a new mobile home on the property for Kelsey. But what a tragedy." Charity clicked her tongue. "Life's short."

"Indeed it is." Steve placed a hand on Kelsey's back, his voice grim. "By the way, this is Kelsey's new wife — Jordyn."

"I didn't know he'd married. Pleased to meet you, Jordyn."

Jordyn!

Kelsey gave a great heave and swung around precariously. Steve grabbed both of his shoulders to steady him.

"Jordyn! It's you!" Kelsey's words were dry in his throat and thick in his mouth. Jordyn stood a few feet away, hands clasped in front of her. Her eyes were shadowed.

Seeing her face cut through his fog. He made to move to her, but got dizzy and fell heavily back on the stool. He grasped at words. "You knew I'd be here, didn't you? I came here because you work here. You work here, right, Jordyn?"

"Oh, Kels." Jordyn's voice broke and a tear rolled down her cheek.

Kelsey's eyes swam. He had hurt her. At a loss, he lifted his arms wide. Steve steadied his body. "C'mere."

Another tear rolled down her cheek as she crossed the few feet between them. She pressed his cheek against her chest and held tight to his head, cradling it. Kelsey leaned heavily against her. His back shook as his tears fell freely onto her breast.

"I'm so sorry." He wound his fingers into the fabric on her back, gripping tightly. "I'm so sorry." Another body racking sob. "So sorry."

She made a soothing sound and pulled him closer.

"Can we?" Jordyn moved an arm above him, asking a question of someone behind him.

"Sure, Hon," Charity replied. "But if I get a customer you guys need to leave. This is definitely bad for business."

"I understand," Jordyn said.

With a sharp sting, a dart pierced through his drunkenness and hit the center of his intoxicated heart. What was it costing Jordyn to be in a brothel with him? He groaned.

"Steve, can you help me?" Jordyn put her hands under Kelsey's arms and lifted. Steve grabbed him sturdily from behind and dragged Kelsey off the bar stool and onto a nearby bench seat. They adjusted him until he lay down, feet on the seat, head on Jordyn's lap.

"I think I can manage now," Jordyn said as she smoothed the hair away from Kelsey's closed eyes.

"Are you sure now?" Steve glanced nervously at Charity, who was examining her nails behind the bar. "What if she needs you to leave?"

"I'm sure. Thank you, Steve." Jordyn's tone was final. "Would you mind checking in on Lizzie and Jeannie? I left them watching the Discovery Channel but I just want to make sure they don't need anything."

"No problem. You call me if you need anything. I mean it. I'll write down my number and put it in Kelsey's truck."

"Thank you."

The weight of her hand felt good on his cheek. It was blissfully quiet; only her soft inhalations and exhalations moved the air around his face. His dry blurry eyes adjusted to the dim room. Kelsey took a moment to examine his surroundings from his cradle on Jordyn's lap. They were alone. Jordyn's head rested back against the wood-paneled wall. Her eyes were closed. A faint crease puckered the skin between her brows. He shifted his weight and her eyes fluttered open.

"Hi," Kelsey said meekly.

"Hi," she replied.

A long silence filled the space between them before Kelsey spoke.

"I'm sorry, Darlin'. I—"

"I know, Kels," Jordyn said, leaning her head back against the wall and searching the darkened ceiling. "I know." She let out her breath on a sigh.

"This is the worst thing I could've done to you." Kelsey felt his heart throbbing and burning as it tore in two. "I'm not a good man."

Jordyn turned her gaze to Kelsey's face and placed a firm hand on each of his cheeks. "Kelsey. I know." She stared hard at him. He searched her eyes for meaning. "You are not a good man." Again, he questioned her silently. She continued, "We obviously can't help being shitty people."

Kelsey opened his mouth to reply but no words came. She spoke for him. "Love, Kels. We have to let love cover all this. We have to let love be enough. Without it, I have no answers. I have nothing but this." She waved a hand around her head to indicate the establishment and situation they were in. Her eyes turned tenderly to his and she leaned down to softly kiss his lips.

"Let love be enough," she whispered against him. "Can you do that one thing?"

Kelsey nodded as a tear rolled down his cheek. "I can." His voice was husky and broken, but his sincerity was strong and unwavering.

She pressed her forehead to his and kissed him again. A tentative smile took over both their features simultaneously.

"If love covers this, it will cover anything," Kelsey said as they pressed their noses together.

"Anything," she said, but paused suddenly over him. "Unless you come back here. It doesn't cover that." Kelsey pulled back. Jordyn giggled softly. "I'm joking. It covers that too." Another pause. "But seriously, don't come here ever again."

Kelsey reached up to cup her cheeks in his hands. "I won't." He looked seriously up at her. "I love you, Darlin." A slow smile brightened her eyes. He answered with his own smile and gently pulled her lips to his.

Jordyn wound an arm under Kelsey's and together they stood up. Within three steps, they reached the door to the brothel. She grasped the solid handle and pulled it open. Kelsey leaned down to leave a lingering kiss on the part in her hair. With a swish of the heavy door, cool desert air filled their lungs. Billions of stars blinked above them in the midnight blue sky. As they turned their faces upward, pricks of light reflecting in their eyes, the door to the brothel swung firmly shut behind them.

Chapter 22

• • • •

KELSEY STARTLED AWAKE from his twenty-year-old memories as a car horn blasted and the driver of a small SUV shouted through his open window, "Get off the road, asshole!" The engine of the SUV accelerated and sped off down the highway.

Kelsey took a deep breath, feeling like he had been sleeping for a solid week. The vividness of his memories made him feel like he had been dreaming. He glanced at the seat next to him.

His daughter, Annalee. Arizona State. The drive home.

Though it wasn't dark yet, the sun was hovering over the hills, heavy with the weight of a full day. Kelsey's body ached from sitting. He rubbed his eyes to clear them. He inhaled deeply, his lungs straining against his ribcage. He adjusted himself on the seat and reached forward to grab the steering wheel. Another SUV sped by, honking obnoxiously. A hand reached from the car's window, middle finger extended. Kelsey flung a curse at the vehicle disappearing into the sunset. Flustered, he turned the key and the '92 shuddered to life. He pushed it into first gear.

Kelsey looked up to check for traffic. He froze. His right foot hovered over the gas pedal.

The sign was faded and decaying. To those who hadn't seen it before, the words were probably not even legible. But Kelsey knew every letter.

Desert Rose Angels.

When Kelsey's foot finally reached the gas pedal and the truck started to inch forward, he pulled it smoothly into the driveway just ten feet away. The sound of his tires on the gravel was startling in its familiarity. As he drew closer to the dilapidated building at the end of the driveway, his stomach began to turn and icy hot sweat beaded on his forehead.

He parked haphazardly in the overgrown parking lot. The white lines that designated parking spaces had long since faded away. His heart thundered in his temples and his fingers tingled.

The truck's door clicked open and Kelsey swung his legs out. His boots stepped onto the gravel, which crunched under his weight. Kelsey took a moment to get his balance and stretch his lower back. Keeping a steady hand on the bed of his truck, he leaned against the bumper and surveyed the brothel.

It had closed ten years ago, though he hadn't heard why. No one had tried to save the building or the property. It hadn't been touched in all those long, hot years. Standing near a place that had been so familiar to him in his younger years made him feel twenty-one again.

Horny as hell and stupider than shit, he thought ruefully. His hand twitched for a cigarette though he had long since quit.

Whispers of his past floated like sage brush through the wind. Faces and places swirled together in a watercolor blur. Floating higher than the rest rose one face.